MINUS MUM

Cardiff Libraries
www.cardiff.gov.uk/libraries

Llyfrgelloedd Caerdyd
www.caerdydd.gov.uk/llyfrgelloedd

US MINUS MUM

Heather Butler

LITTLE, BROWN BOOKS FOR YOUNG READERS
www.lbkids.co.uk

LITTLE, BROWN BOOKS FOR YOUNG READERS

First published in Great Britain in 2014 by
Little, Brown Books for Young Readers
This paperback edition published in 2015 by Hodder & Stoughton

5 7 9 10 8 6 4

A CIP catalogue record for this book
is available from the British Library.

ISBN 978-0-349-12407-0

Typeset in Stone Serif by M Rules
Printed and bound in Great Britain by
Clays Ltd, St Ives plc

The paper and board used in this book are
made from wood from responsible sources.

MIX
Paper from
responsible sources
FSC® C104740

Little, Brown Books for Young Readers
An imprint of
Hachette Children's Group
and published by Hodder & Stoughton
338 Euston Road, London NW1 3BH

An Hachette UK Company
www.hachette.co.uk

www.lbkids.co.uk

Dedicated to
Joyce Jelbart
(1922 – 2011)

Mongrel means your parents are not the same breed.

We are on our way to look at a dog.

'Mr and Mrs Warren?' the man says.

Mum nods.

Dad nods.

Theo nods. He is holding Mum's hand because he has never been to a Dog Rescue Centre before.

Everyone else is nodding and I don't want to be left out, so I nod as well.

Then we follow the man to a cage. There is a sign on the door.

It says . . .

1

**Pong & Ping.
Mongrels.
Keep together
if possible.**

'Here they are,' the man says. He lifts them both out. Pong shuffles back towards the cage. Ping doesn't. He climbs all over us and is soft, and his tail thumps against our legs and Theo says,

'I want this one.'

'What do you think, George?' Dad says. And it's like Ping knows I've been asked to make a decision about him. So he stops licking Theo's trousers, looks at me and blinks very slowly.

Twice.

So I say,

'I want him as well.'

'Ping it is then,' Mum says. 'Which is great because Nana and Granddad want Pong.'

The man from the Dog Rescue Centre smiles.

'We're happy for them to go to different homes,' he says, 'as long as they still see each other.'

'They will definitely do that,' Mum says.

Because Nana and Granddad come to visit us quite often.

So Ping comes to live with us and Mum calls him
Goffo.

And Pong goes to live with Nana and Granddad
and is known as **Ivan the Terrible**. Only he
doesn't stay terrible for long because Nana takes
him to Dog Training Classes where Mrs Rentop teaches
him to be a good dog.

So now he is just called Ivan.

Dermo has a **snazzy** new lunch box. He puts it on the trolley outside our classroom next to my scruffy old one. Then we go in the classroom and sit down. Morning work is on the board. It's there to give us something to do while Mrs Logan takes the register and sorts herself out.

On your whiteboards, write words using letters in the word FIREWORKS.

Only I can't write anything because my whiteboard pen has disappeared.

So I ask Mrs Logan for a new one.

And she tells me to check my pencil case.

So I do, and it's still not there.

Dermo looks and he can't see it either.

'I still can't find my pen,' I tell Mrs Logan.

'Mmmmmm,' she says, opening her special
drawer. 'Look after this one.' The pen she gives
me is new because no one has chewed the top.

'Thank you,' I say, and smile at her.

And she smiles back.

I try my pen out by drawing a picture of an alien
with six teeth and a spike sticking out of his
bottom. The spike was meant to be a tail, but it
went a bit wrong. Dermo writes forks on his white
board, so I write *forks* down as well, underneath
my alien. Then I whisper,

'Wires and fires.'

And while we make up words, Mrs Logan takes
the register.

'Hello, Miriam,' she says.

'Hello, Mrs Logan,' Miriam says back.

'Hello, Kit.'

'Hello, Mrs Logan.'

'Hello, George.'

And I say,

'Hello, Mrs Logan.'

'Hello, Carl.'

Silence.

My eyes swivel towards his chair.

He is definitely away.

Then AJ Rivers says,

'His cat was run over last night. By a lorry.'

And Mrs Logan says,

'That's probably why he's away then.'

And even though I don't like Carl, I still feel a little bit sad for him.

After the register it is science. Today we are looking at hot water.

Mrs Logan gives each table a polystyrene and a plastic cup. Then she hands out china mugs with

Watson Park Primary

written on them and it is great because Carl Worthington doesn't lean over and grab them. He sits by himself on a table next to ours and works with us when we do things like this.

Which none of us like.

Because he takes our pencil sharpeners without asking.

And copies our work.

And says stupid things.

And belches.

And pulls bogeys out of his nose.

And is always getting in trouble.

Which is why he sits on a table on his own.

Only he's not here today and Mrs Logan is pouring exactly one hundred millilitres of boiled water in each cup. We have to measure the water temperature every five minutes and draw a graph to show which cools the quickest. On my graph, the polystyrene cup is the brown line, the plastic one is violet and the china mug is red. Dermo uses the same colours. Alice and Skye, who sit opposite us, use light pink, dark pink and red.

Because they are girls.

We do three measurements and then Skye knocks the polystyrene cup over. So now there is water on our pencil cases and Alice's sweatshirt. If Carl Worthington had done that, we'd have made a fuss.

But today we just giggle and Dermo and I find some paper towels and Alice asks Mrs Logan for some more water so we can start again.

And as we do, an idea pops into my brain.

It is a brilliant idea.

We won't be able to do it until Saturday.

It's to do with Goffo.

And I can't wait to tell Theo.

Because he will think that my idea is hilarious.*

*Hilarious is my favourite word at the moment.

We buy **pig's ears** from Purrfect Pet Shop, which is
next to the opticians in town. Dogs chew them
once a week to keep their teeth and gums healthy.
But when Chelsea are on the telly, if Goffo growls at
them, Dad gives him an extra one. Goffo loves
pig's ears so much, he now growls at:

- anyone wearing a blue Chelsea football shirt

- parked cars that are blue

- Dermo's front door

- the blue flower pots on our patio.

11

'Jack, why did you start this?' Mum says. 'It's ridiculous! That dog is bad enough without you making him worse.'

'I'm training him to wag his tail every time he hears the word "Arsenal" next,' Dad says.

And Mum says,

'Promise me. You are not going to use pig's ears for that. Goffo's only meant to have them for a special treat.'

'But he likes them,' Dad says.

And we are all laughing, because while they are talking, Goffo chases round the room throwing a pig's ear in the air and catching it like it is a ball. Only then he misses and the pig's ear shoots under the sofa.

He tries to stick his nose under the sofa.

Only his nose is too big.

So he gives up and looks sad and scratches his tummy instead.

Which makes wind **spurt** out of his little bottom.

And that makes us laugh even more.

'You're a daft dog,' Dad says to him.

And Dad's right. Goffo is.

Mum and Dad have banned the word ending in art and starting with fffff ... because it makes Theo giggle so much he nearly wets himself.

Pig's ears make Goffo pass **squelchy, stinky wind** and when he does a real **whopper of a wifta**, while the smell hangs in the air, he shuffles backwards waving his nose like a **vacuum cleaner** trying to suck it back in again.

Ivan never has pig's ears because Nana does not find wind funny.

That is because she is a teacher.

Mum works in The Flower Shop in town and Dad designs ejection seats for aeroplanes, so they find wind a little bit funny.

14

Theo and I think anything to do with wind is brilliantly hilarious.

Anyway, it is Saturday morning and Theo and I have an experiment to do. Mum is having a lie-in and Dad is reading the newspaper. So Theo and I tiptoe to the garage where the tin with the pig's ears lives, on the shelf next to the window.

Goffo is lying on the patio thinking about rabbits. But when he sees us, he turns his nose like a **periscope** on a submarine and sniffs, loudly. Then he stands up and bounces towards Theo's left hand.

'Other side of the shed,' I whisper to him. 'Come on.'

At exactly eleven o'clock on the morning of Saturday 16th November, Goffo is given a pig's ear. He fights with it like it is trying to escape, then tries to sink his teeth into it. And exactly ten minutes later we pull the pig's ear out of his mouth, take it to the garage and put it back in the tin. Goffo follows us looking sad.

'You're not having any more,' I tell him, 'but you must stay with us, all day, because you are part of an important experiment.'

That afternoon, at six minutes past five, as Theo's Lego pirate ship blasts into outer space and I am reading page fifty-seven of my book, Goffo sends out a massive **gust** of squidgy, smelly wind. Then he shuffles backwards breathing in the smell.

As he does, Theo says,

'That's the pig's ear one.'

And I agree.

That one was the big one we've been waiting for.

So now we know, because we have **scientifically** proved it, that when Goffo chews a pig's ear for ten minutes, it takes six hours and six minutes before he does a whopping wifta, which is easy to remember.

The only person we tell this scientific discovery to is Natters because she is our cousin and is eleven and in Year Six, which is one year above me and three years above Theo. She doesn't go to our school and her mum, who is called Chrissie, is our mum's big sister. They come round to our house all the time.

When we tell Natters, she says,

'Someone at school said people **fart*** fourteen times a day. Are dogs the same?'

'Don't know,' I say. And Theo says,

'Does Nana do fourteen wiftas every day as well?' And his knees are twitching and his face has gone bright red because he is trying so hard not to giggle. 'Next time she and Granddad visit,' he says, 'I'm going to stay near Nana's bottom and count them.'

Knowing Theo, he will, as well.

*Natters is allowed to use that word because Mum and Dad have only banned me and Theo from using it.

FACT NUMBER SEVEN

Mum and Dad say we are lucky having Mrs Shardini as our neighbour because we could have someone who kept skunks or who didn't like children living next door.

Dad builds a wooden fence to stop **Goffo** escaping from our garden. You can tell **Goffo** loves the fence because sometimes he licks it after he has weed on it.

We live at number 47, Holly Tree Road and are on a corner.

Mrs Shardini lives at number 49.

She does not love **Goffo**.

At all.

Theo and I call her Mrs Shardini because she works in a **laboratory**. She goes swimming every Wednesday and hangs a pink **bikini** and a blue towel on the washing line, even in winter. Theo is making up a limerick. It goes like this ...

> There once was a Mrs Shardini
> Who wore a pink bikini,
> She had a big **dimple**
> And hair with a **pimple** ...

Theo cannot think of the last line, so his limerick is a **work in progress**. The last line is always the hardest to think of. Mum and Dad call her Irenie because they are adults and have facial hair. Mum uses **tweezers** to pull hairs out of her eyebrows.

And her nose.

I watched her do it the other day.

In the bathroom.

One day I will shave.

So will Theo.

But neither of us do at the moment.

When our football goes over the fence and into Mrs Shardini's garden, we climb on the bird table Nana gave Mum last year. It is usually Theo who does the climbing because adults think he is cute. Mum says the table is for birds and not for boys. So we make sure she is not in the kitchen or back room before he stands on it.

If Mrs Shardini is in her garden, and she often is because she loves gardening, Theo says,

'Hello, Mrs Shardini, can we have our ball back, please?'

And she always smiles and says, 'Hello,' and asks what he is doing.

It is obvious what he is doing. He is standing on a bird table looking over the fence asking for his ball back, but he tells her about something else he is doing, because Mum and Dad want us to always be polite.

When Mrs Shardini throws our ball back she tries to get it in the trampoline cage and we tell her if it goes in.

Then we carry on playing football until the ball goes back in her garden again.

FACT NUMBER EIGHT

The flower called Lobelia is named after Matthias de Lobel who lived in Belgium.

Mum and I sometimes stand looking out of my bedroom window. She says that one day, our back garden will be like Mrs Shardini's, with lots of flowers and a beautiful lawn and maybe a water feature. But for now, she'll make do with the front garden so Theo and Goffo and I can have the back.

So we stare over the fence into Mrs Shardini's and Mum tells me the names of the different flowers she's planted and we play the **Visiting Game** which goes like this.

Mum says,

'A lady visits a garden and sees ... a sunflower.'

And I have to say something about whatever the person sees or does.

So for a sunflower I might say,

'Van Gogh,' because he was a man who painted a picture with sunflowers in it.

Or I might say, 'Yellow'.

Sometimes I say two or three things.

So if Mum says,

'The lady visits a garden and sees ... Lobelia,' I say,

'Lobelia are named after Matthias de Lobel. They can be blue or red or white or purple.'

And so on.

We play the **Visiting Game** with capital cities as well. So Mum says, 'A young man visits ... France.'

And I say, 'Paris.'

'His friend visits ... **Maseru**'. And that is from a list of countries and capital cities Mum downloaded from the internet. So I say,

'**Lesotho.**'

And Mum says,

'You are so clever.'

Sometimes we play with dinosaur names.

Or cars.

Or animals.

Or anything.

The **Visiting Game** is something only Mum and I play. Theo doesn't like learning new words like I do and Dad doesn't get home until eight o'clock in the evening. All he does then is eat his supper and sleep in front of the television. Mum and I play other games as well, like Scrabble or hangman or seeing who can wave the fastest. She is dead good at waving.

Last week she did sixteen waves in five seconds.

FACT NUMBER NINE

Mum's roast potatoes are scrumptious and delicious.

Goffo wants to visit Mrs Shardini's garden and see what's there, so he starts digging holes like he is making a tunnel. He **lives with failure** until one Sunday when the rest of us are eating **roast dinner**.

Mum's mobile rings.

She ignores it and carries on telling us about her aerobics class and the new lady called Precious Pearson, who speaks fluent Chinese.

Theo pours gravy over his carrots to make them look like **orange islands in a brown sea**.

Dad reaches for the tomato ketchup.

I dig my fork into a **crispy** roast potato.

Mum's mobile rings again.

'I'd better get that,' she sighs.

'Goffo's done what ... ?' she says. 'Irenie, I am so sorry. He's dug underneath ... Irenie, I'll be round straight away ...'

'Naughty dog,' Dad whispers. 'Mum should have taken him to Dog Training Classes like Nana said.'

Mum flips her phone shut.

'Stupid animal,' she says. 'He's barking at her and she is terrified.'

'Good thing she had her mobile with her,' Dad says, 'or she could have been stuck there for hours with a **lunatic dog** watching her every move.'

As soon as Mum is out of the door, Dad says,

'Quick. Let's see what's going on.'

So we race upstairs and line up along my bedroom window. And there's Mrs Shardini and she is wearing ... a blue skirt. And Goffo doesn't understand why she is waving her arms in the air and thinks she is playing **Waving Windmills** like Theo and I play with him. Only she's not. And Goffo's making a lot of noise but there is no way he would ever hurt her.

A minute later, Mum walks down the garden waving Goffo's pink lead. Goffo races round Mrs Shardini once more, then crouches low on the grass.

'He's ...' Theo breathes with **awe in his voice**, 'he's ... doing a ... in the middle of Mrs Shardini's garden.'

Goffo's tail is up, his funny little nose is stretched out and we watch poo **slither gracefully** out of his bottom.

'That dog is so embarrassing,' Dad says and we are all giggling. Then Theo says in his limerick voice,

'On Mrs Shardini's lawn.'

And Dad carries on,

'On a chilly winter's morn.' And that is a bit posh, but it doesn't matter because I already have the next two lines in my head, and they end with Theo's favourite rhyming words,

'A dog did a poo, and not in a loo.'

And then there's silence and we are all trying to come up with the last line that ends with an 'awn' sound.

'Can't think of anything,' I say and I'm running through the alphabet trying to think of words that will fit, like 'born' and 'dawn' and 'Shaun'.

But my brain has gone blank.

So has Theo's.

So has Dad's.

'It's another work in progress,' Dad says.

In the afternoon, Dad fills in the hole under the fence and Mum bakes some of her special chocolate cookies. She takes them, and Theo, round to Mrs Shardini to apologise for Goffo. Theo is meant to make Mrs Shardini smile and feel happy. Only he has mud on his shoes.

And walks all over her brand new carpet.

FACT NUMBER TEN

Dermo Harris is my very best friend.

Today, Dermo and I are wearing the same T-shirts because it's the school Christmas party so we are not in school uniform.

We take our coats off, then point at each other.

And laugh.

When we walk in the classroom, Mrs Logan laughs too.

'Is there anything you don't do together?' she says.

And we shake our heads.

'We didn't plan this,' Dermo says.

We're just best friends.

Our mums are best friends as well.

Carl Worthington has a bandage on his knee because he hit a tree root and fell off his bike at the dips in **Squire Wood**. His mum has sent a letter to school asking if he can sit on a chair in assembly because his knee hurts when he bends it. He won't be out in the playground today either.

His mum's going to buy him a new bike for Christmas, with a seven speed chainset and twenty-four inch wheels. He's getting a new iPad as well.

I haven't even got an iPad, let alone a new one.

But we don't live in Shaftesbury Lane.

And Carl Worthington does.

My main Christmas present is a new bed, a new wardrobe and a new carpet in my bedroom. Dad started decorating my room last weekend. We went to town and I helped choose some green paint and a new quilt cover with an **Arsenal cannon** on it.

Carl Worthington's jacket creaks when he moves because it is made of real leather. His dad brought it back from Spain last time he was playing golf out there. Carl fiddles with the studs round the collar as Mrs Logan takes the register and everyone else works out different ways Santa's elves can load their sleigh. It's a maths challenge and I make a mistake and need to change a five to a three. My rubber's not in my pencil case and it's the one Nana bought when we went on the London Eye last year.

So Dermo lends me his.

We are doing Christmas decorations.

All morning.

Everyone is going to make a crown, a name badge and a Christmas tree decoration. Mrs Fraser, who is our Teaching Assistant, is decorating cardboard stockings with glitter and sticky paper and will call us to her table when she is ready.

Mum and Theo and I often sit at the kitchen table and make sticky things. We made elephants last night by cutting the tops off plastic milk bottles. The highest bit of the handle became the trunk. Then we stuck paper all over them. We're going to decorate them tonight. Theo wants to do his in coloured squares like Elmer. I'm going to make mine grey, but give him a gold medal because he's just won the triathlon in the **Elephant Olympics**.

Dermo covers his crown with gold paper. So does Alice. I am about to start my crown when Carl Worthington leans over and grabs all the gold paper. As he does, he stares at me and smirks. I hate it when he does that because he wants me to ask him, to beg him, for some gold paper.

Only I am not going to.

Because if I do, he wins.

And I do not want him to win.

So I use shiny red paper instead and draw a cannon in black felt-tipped pen.

And my crown is the best because it is an Arsenal crown.

And Carl Worthington's crown is the worst because he is rubbish at cutting and sticking.

FACT NUMBER ELEVEN

If you get a red card, your mum is phoned and told how naughty you have been. I have never ever had one of those.

I am drawing a second cannon when Mrs Fraser calls us to her table to decorate the stockings.

'There is enough, but you'll have to be careful with the glitter,' she says as we sit down.

Carl Worthington picks up the pot with the glitter in.

'That's got to go round five of you,' Mrs Fraser says to him.

'Yeah, we get it,' Carl says. 'We're not stupid.'

'I'm going to ignore that comment,' Mrs Fraser says, 'but, Carl, think about what you say. And can

32

you put the glitter down, please. You've got to cut the stocking out before decorating it.'

He puts the pot on the table, in front of where he is sitting.

'Carl, put the pot in the middle of the table, please,' Mrs Fraser says.

Skye and Alice and Dermo and I watch. Our eyes **dart** between Carl Worthington's and Mrs Fraser's face.

'I've put it on the table, haven't I?' he says, and his voice is so rude.

'You, young man, can go back to your place,' Mrs Fraser says. 'You are not going to speak to me like that.'

And Carl Worthington says,

'I haven't done anything.'

'Back to your place.'

'Make me,' Carl Worthington says and Skye and Dermo and Alice and I are all thinking,

Go on, Mrs Fraser. You can do it. Get rid of him.

But he gets rid of himself because he suddenly picks up the pot of glitter upside down and scatters it all over the floor. And as he does, he stares at Mrs Fraser like she is a **maggot's toenail**.

'Mrs Logan,' Mrs Fraser calls across the classroom. 'We have a code D in the warehouse.'

Mrs Logan walks across the classroom to the table, takes one look at the floor, the glitter, the empty pot, Carl Worthington's face, our **shocked and disgusted expressions**, Mrs Fraser's eyes which are bulging out of their sockets, and says,

'Green card. Now. And don't bother coming back to this table. You had your chance and you're not spoiling today for everyone else.'

Carl Worthington stands up and kicks his chair so it **topples over**.

'And you can pick that chair up as well,' Mrs Logan adds.

'Make me,' he says.

And now everyone in the class is staring at him as Mrs Logan says,

'That is an orange card. And you are so nearly on a red one.' And all Carl does is shrug as he walks over to where the cards are kept. He's going to have to fill out a form now and say what he did and how he is going to improve his behaviour.

Mrs Fraser sighs and bends over to try and recycle some of the glitter. And we don't mind if she doesn't save any of it, because we can decorate our stockings in peace. I shall make mine red and draw another cannon on it.

Today is an Arsenal day, and they'd better win when they play Man. City tonight.

Dad wins an **inflatable, plastic reindeer** at work. He blows it up and puts it by the Christmas tree in the front room. Goffo thinks the reindeer is real and will play with him.

Only it doesn't.

So Goffo looks sad and scratches his ears, and as he does, Theo shouts,

'Silver Peugeot alert.'

'Goffo,' Dad says, 'I know it's **Christmas Day**, but Elise is here and she does not like you. So you're off to the bottom of the garden. But I promise we'll get you in as soon as she's gone.'

Then he adds,

'Nana doesn't like you much either, does she?'
And he gives Goffo a cuddle as he carries him
towards the back door.

At least it's not raining or snowing.

We met Elise at half term. She wore a pale blue
jumper and waved her arms every time Goffo
went near her. He thought she was playing
Waving Windmills, so went near her an awful
lot.

Anyway, Mum is walking to the front door, Dad is
sticking Goffo out of the back door and Theo is in
the front room singing,

'Elise, Elise, you make me sneeze, your feet are
smelly and look like cheese.'

And then he shouts,

'Fourteen!' and we both start giggling.

'Happy Christmas,' Grandpa says as Dad opens
the front door. He leans forward and whispers,
'Where's Goffo?'

'In the garden,' Dad whispers back.

Grandpa turns round and calls out. 'Elise, it's OK. You can get out of the car.'

We stand in a line to say 'Happy Christmas' to each other.

'I'm sure you've grown,' Elise says as her **ruby red suckers** brush over my cheek. Theo and I must teach her how to high-five us. That is far better than a **vampire slurp** dribbling over our faces.

'And how are you, **my little Dragon Slayer?**' Grandpa says as he leans his walking stick against the radiator. I hold my arms out and he lifts me up, kisses my forehead, tells me I am one of his favourite grandchildren, then puts me down again.

'Yup. I can still pick you up,' he says.

'Please, no one in the back room,' Mum says, 'or Goffo will throw himself through the patio window.'

'I do feel bad about him being outside,' Elise says.

'Oh don't worry,' Mum laughs. 'He'll survive.'
Then she says, 'Boys, take Elise in the front room
while I make coffee. Why don't you show her the
elephants we made?'

So in the front room we go.

FACT NUMBER THIRTEEN

Elise's real name is Elisabeth Clutterbuck.

Elise is a pencil sharpener designer who has never had children. She met Grandpa last summer when she tripped over a rug in a carpet shop. He helped her up and they fell in love. Her website has a picture of a pencil sharpener that looks like a teapot. The pencil goes in the spout and makes a rumbling noise like a kettle boiling when the lead has a sharp point.

Dad's real mum died when I was three. There's a photograph of her on the wall behind the door in the back room. Theo is in his buggie and I'm **clutching** a fire engine. So I can sort of remember her.

But not that well.

Elise sits in Dad's chair and we show her Elmer and Usain Elephant.

'Wow!' she says. 'They are beautiful.' And she balances them on her knees like they are talking to each other.

'I love elephants,' she says.

'Do you know how to tell the difference between an Indian and an African elephant?' I ask her.

'Go on, tell me,' she says, and I say,

'An Indian elephant's ears are shaped like India.'

And she nods her head and says,

'That's a clever way of remembering it.'

Then she says,

'I know this might sound stupid, but I don't know what people your age do all day.'

So Theo tells her about Matthew Draylong's tooth falling out when he was eating a cheese sandwich and about being the back of a camel in the school play and falling over just before he went on stage. Then he asks if she wants to see his dinosaurs.

'They sound interesting,' she says.

So he fetches them and we clear the coffee table of its books and coasters and magazines and Theo lines them up on it and counts them. He has eighteen altogether.

Elise can see what they look like because she wears purple glasses, but Theo says,

'This one's a **Patagosaurus**.'

'A what?'

'A Patagosaurus. It's got a green neck and a very, very little head and it kills the other dinosaurs like this.' And he **whams** the plastic dinosaur against the arm of the chair several times.

'They're all dead now,' he carries on, 'so he's going to have his breakfast. Then their mummies will cook sausages on a barbecue and they'll have tomato sauce made out of blood. And this one is called **Edmontania**.'

Theo is talking a load of rubbish, but Elise says,

'There are so many new dinosaur names these days. Where do they get them from?'

'The internet,' Theo says. 'You can get anything on there. These spikes, here, they could kill you.' And he holds Edmontania in front of her face.

'Shall we look at the other dinosaurs?' Elise says, moving Theo's hand away from her nose.

Theo's dinosaurs once belonged to me but I don't play with them any more, so he has them.

Except for my **Triceratops**.

Chrissie bought him for me and he lives on top of the drawers by my bed, next to my new Arsenal lamp.

Elise leans over and opens her bag.

'I bought this book the other day,' she says. 'It's a poem called *The Night Before Christmas*, and it's about a house where no one is stirring, not even a mouse. Shall I read it to you? It's got pop-ups to look at as well.'

Theo nods because he likes being read to and he likes poems and he likes pop-up books. And I nod because Elise is trying really hard to do things she thinks we will be interested in.

'My mother used to read this to me and my little brother every Christmas Eve,' she says.

'Where's your mother now?' Theo says.

'In heaven.'

'Is she dead, then?'

'She is.'

'And where's your little brother?'

'He's in heaven too.'

'Is he dead as well?'

'He is.'

'And where's your daddy?'

'I don't know.'

'Have you got anyone else?'

'No,' she says, 'but I do have your grandpa and he is very special. And there are two boys and a family in this house to think about. And I also have lots of very nice friends.'

Mrs Logan says people are always more interesting than just nice. But I don't tell Elise that because she has started reading the poem and Theo is getting ready to pull Santa's sleigh across the page.

'Thank you,' she says when she finishes the poem and smiles at us as she closes the book. Then she

slides it into her bag and takes out a pair of earrings. Each is a six-pointed star with flashing lights that change colour.

'Would your mum like these?' she says. 'I made them for her, but I wanted to check with you first to make sure they'd be all right.'

Mum loves **whacky** things so we say they will be OK.

'I must put them under the tree before she comes back in then,' she says, and Theo and I watch as Elise drops the earrings in a little box with a bow on it.

As she does, Goffo goes **completely mental**.

FACT NUMBER FIFTEEN

Dogs can smell each other round corners.

Even though Nana washes Ivan in his special doggie bath, it doesn't get rid of his smell.

And Goffo has smelt his brother.

Theo and I look out of the window. Nana and Granddad's white Fiesta is on our drive. A **whisper of a woof** comes from the front garden followed by **hysterical howls** from the back.

'They are so sweet,' Theo says. 'They're talking to each other.'

'Is that another dog arriving?' Elise says.

'Goffo's brother,' Theo says. 'Lives with Nana and

Granddad. Huge teeth, sharp claws, bites, jumps, scratches, eats people.'

Elise's **cheeks vibrate with terror**.

'Ignore Theo,' I say. 'Nana took Ivan to Dog Training Classes. He doesn't move or do anything. He's not like a real dog.'

'Are you sure?' she says.

'I'm sure,' I say. 'If Nana tells him, he will ignore you.'

Ivan is like **Robot Dog** with Nana at the controls. He stays next to her as she and Granddad come in the front room. Grandpa comes in too, carrying a plate of **chocolate biscuits**. And everyone kisses each other and says 'Happy Christmas' and laughs.

'Ivan is staying with me,' Nana tells Mum. 'If he goes outside, his brother will teach him bad manners and he might catch a cold.'

'Goffo isn't that bad!' Mum says.

'Listen to him,' Nana says and pauses **dramatically**. Everyone stops what they are doing and listens to Goffo scratching the patio window and whining. 'Vicky, he needs Dog Training Classes,' Nana says. 'See Ivan? I could take him anywhere.'

She is right.

She could.

You don't even know Ivan is in the room.

He does not move or bark or scratch or twitch or do blow-offs or anything.

Unless Nana says he can.

And today she has said he can't.

'It is Christmas Day and I don't want to talk about it,' Mum says. 'You've trained Ivan how you want him to be and we've trained Goffo how we want him to be. Let's just leave it at that.'

Elise looks at me and her eyes widen.

And then we both smile at each other.

'Anyone for a biscuit?' Grandpa says, and suddenly everyone starts talking again and the sofa and the armchairs are full of people and Elise is returning Elmer and Usain back to the mantelpiece next to a card with baby Jesus on it and Mum is putting coasters on the coffee table.

'Ivan, sit,' Nana says. And he bends his back legs and sits next to her left foot.

'He is so well trained now,' she says, looking at Mum who ignores her.

'And how many presents do you think are under the tree?' Nana says to Theo as he **plonks his bottom** next to hers on the sofa.

'Ffffourteen,' he says in a loud voice and sticks his tongue out at me. 'Ffffourteen,' he says again. 'I won.' And he wriggles his bottom towards the edge of the sofa so his body is lying across the seat. Then he buries his face in the cushion Nana is sitting on.

'Theo, what are you doing?' Nana says to him, and Theo lifts his face up and says,

'Pretending to be a mole.' And Nana looks at him like he is a **salted peanut** and says,

'If you want to be a mole, go and sit by your granddad. He doesn't mind you wriggling and scratching around next to him. But if you sit next to me, you sit sensibly and stop being a mole.'

And I know Theo will do what Nana has told him, because what Nana says, everyone does.

Natters and Chrissie arrive ten minutes later. So
while the adults drink coffee and talk about
grown up things, Theo, Natters and I go down the
garden to give Goffo his Christmas present.

When Goffo smells it, he spins round three times
and says,

'Ruff, ruff,' which means 'Thank you for my pig's
ear.'

'Happy Christmas,' Theo says.

'And in six hours and six minutes,' Natters says,
'we will make sure you are inside the house
spending time with your brother.'

And Theo starts singing,

'Pig's ears, pig's ears, good for your heart, pig's ears, pig's ears, they make you ... **fffffffff** ...'

'Shush!' Natters says, 'or I will have to take you to Dog Training Classes.'

'I was going to say fffffffffourteen,' he says.

'You weren't,' I say.

'Was,' he says.

And we all know he wasn't. He was going to say the word fffffffart.*

*I haven't actually said it, so that word is allowed to be written down.

53

Three days after Christmas I go to Dermo's for a
sleepover. His dressing gown smells of Marmite
and mine smells of salt and vinegar crisps. We are
eating **caramel flavoured popcorn** and **Maltesers**
and playing on his PlayStation. His mum, who's
called Sharon, says we can stay up all night if we
want, as long as we don't keep her awake.

So we are being very quiet.

'Dad's girlfriend's having a baby,' Dermo
suddenly says.

A bit of popcorn drops out of his fingers and
sticks to his dressing gown. He picks it up and
sticks it in his mouth. 'He's never going to get
back with Mum. He's moving to Australia as well.'

And all I can think to say is,

'That's miles away.'

And I imagine what it would be like if my mum and dad split up and then Dad went to live in Australia.

It would be horrible.

'Dad said I wasn't to tell Mum until he had gone,' Dermo says.

'Why?'

'He doesn't want her charging round to their house making a fuss, because it will upset Fiona.'

'So why did he tell you?'

'He didn't. A man came round to buy their sofa, and they thought I was upstairs. Only I was in the kitchen, and I heard them telling him. So I asked Dad about it. And he said they were going. At the end of January.'

'And are you going to tell your mum?'

He shrugs.

'Dunno,' he says. Then he goes,

'Promise, promise, promise not to tell.'

And I high-five him and say in a robot sort of voice,

'Promise will be kept.'

Because that's what we always say when we tell each other things we don't want anyone else to know about.

We sit in silence for a few seconds.

Then he says,

'I might never see my dad again because it costs loads to get to Australia and Mum can't afford it.'

'Won't your dad pay for you to go out and see him?'

'Dunno.'

We finish the popcorn and most of the Maltesers and play on until our game is at a save point.

'I'm tired,' Dermo says.

I am as well.

So I get under my quilt and Henry Snail is waiting for me.

And Dermo gets under his quilt and Chip is waiting for him.

Henry Snail and Chip say 'goodnight' to each other like they always do. And as we hide them back under our quilts, Dermo says,

'Imagine what Carl would say if he was here.'

'He wouldn't be here,' I say.

'But do you think he still has a cuddly?' Dermo says. And I've never thought about Carl Worthington having a cuddly.

'Bet he does,' I say. 'But he'd never tell anyone.'

And we are both under our quilts and we both know we will carry on whispering, even though it is twenty to three in the morning.

FACT NUMBER NINETEEN

He shouldn't, but Dermo's dad tells lies.

It is snowing the first day back after the Christmas holidays. Mrs Logan lets us put our gloves on the radiator. And Miss Cortez says we can have an **extra ten minutes playtime** if we wrap up and no one throws snowballs or makes slides.

I'm glad we're doing something fun because Dermo's dad and Fiona left yesterday even though it is not the end of January, but the very beginning. They told Sharon on New Year's Day. She and Dermo came straight round to our house because Sharon couldn't stop crying. It was like when Dermo's dad first left. She was round all the time then.

'I just can't believe he's done it,' she sobbed. 'He knows I can't afford to stick Dermo on aeroplanes.'

'He might send some money,' Mum said. 'Dermo is his son.'

'He won't,' Sharon said. 'I reckon Fiona's pregnant and they're going to start their new little family as far away from their old life as possible.'

Then Mum said,

'Does Dermo know if she's pregnant?'

'He hasn't said anything.'

I looked at Dermo.

Dermo looked at me.

Neither of us said a word. We just carried on building our **Technic Lego excavator** in silence so we could hear what was going on in the kitchen.

Today Dermo needs something to cheer him up because he didn't even get to see his dad before he left. So we make a snowman with Kit and Skye and Riz.

And before long the playground looks like a family of **white dwarf** aliens have landed.

FACT NUMBER TWENTY

Teachers at Watson Park Primary School are learning how to teach maths. They can't do it if children are there, so we have a day off and meet Nana and Granddad at Topplehurst Model Village.

Nana teaches Year Two on a Thursday and a Friday. Jason Mollens is in her class. He is a **pain in the neck** and has a star chart to make him behave. But today he will not annoy her because it is a Monday and Nana is with Granddad and they are with us.

We **officially love** Topplehurst Model Village. It costs ten pounds per family to enter, and dogs are allowed in if they are on a lead. Everything is one tenth the size it would be in real life and children can climb wherever they want. It takes twenty-three minutes to get to from our house and has a heated picnic area in a sort of greenhouse. So even though it is February, we are having a picnic and Mum has made some cheese straws for a treat.

When we arrive at the model village, Granddad and Nana are not in the car park.

'Do you think Ivan was a naughty boy and slowed them down?' Mum says. And I say,

'That dog wouldn't dare be naughty.'

Then Mum says,

'Nana visits a garage and buys ... a **Ferrari**.'

And I say,

'Sports car. Italian.'

And as I say the word 'Italian', a white Fiesta **zooms** into the car park. Granddad is driving. If Nana was driving, the car would have **glided**. Goffo jumps in the air, hits his head on the bars at the top of the cage and starts howling with excitement.

'He's thinking about Ivan's bottom,' Theo says.

'He's not,' Mum says.

'He is,' Theo says.

'There are fffffourteen leaves on that tree. Beat you!' I say.

'Bet she did one in the car and didn't tell Granddad,' Theo says and we are both giggling.

'What are you two giggling about?' Mum says.

'Nothing,' Theo says, and I say

'The number fourteen.'

'Sounds like you're being a bit rude,' Mum says and she is looking straight at us.

'No I'm not,' Theo says, which really means 'Yes I am.' And Mum says,

'Whatever it is, stop it.'

The dogs sniff each other for a few minutes while Nana and Granddad get themselves out of their car and put on their coats. When they are ready, Nana says,

'Ivan, heel.'

And Ivan freezes then trots over to where Nana is standing. And it is like her dark green skirt is full of **magnets** and he is made out of metal.

Mum tries to do the same with Goffo.

'Goffo, sit,' she says. And Goffo jumps and woofs even more and then tries to bury his nose under his brother's bottom, which is now on the white line next to Nana's brown shoe. Ivan moves his head towards Goffo in a **jerky twitch**, as if he is blowing him a kiss.

'He'll calm down in a minute,' Mum says.

'I certainly hope he does,' Nana says. Then she adds, 'Good boy,' to Ivan who gives a little 'ruff' like he is talking back to her.

He is so sweet.

Last time we came here it was Nana's birthday and we had lunch at an expensive restaurant where waiters wear bowties and hold trays in the air. I had **wild boar with honey sauce** and it was yummy and Nana said I was very grown up to try something like that from the adult menu.

Today it is no one's birthday, so that's why we're having a picnic.

Granddad and I travel in an **anti-clockwise**
direction, with Goffo and Ivan. We have a lead
each and as soon as Nana is out of sight, the dogs
sniff and lick each other then run off in opposite
directions.

Theo, Nana and Mum walk round the village in a
clockwise direction. We will meet them at the
greenhouse lunch place because that is **halfway**
round. Then Theo will carry on with Mum, the dogs
and Granddad (who will **double back** on himself)
and I will go with Nana (who will also double back).
That way, our grandparents spend time with each of
us and Mum makes sure Theo behaves himself.

Dad is not with us because he is the only person in the world who knows how the ejection seat on a new aeroplane works. So his boss, who is called Keith, has sent him to a boring meeting in Birmingham. Last year, Keith sent Dad to Japan where they have jet lag and the capital city is Tokyo. Mum went with him and Dad bought her a dress with pink cherry blossom all over it. She keeps it in a special plastic bag in her wardrobe. Theo and I stayed with Sharon and Dermo and it was wicked. We had a midnight feast every night and Theo slept in his new sleeping bag.

Anyway, the first three things Granddad and I see are:

- model pirate ship
- submarine
- forest with trees

Each tree in the forest has a wooden ladder and **shafts of light pierce** through slits cut in the plastic trunks. I always climb to the top and sit on the seat carved into the branches. Today when I am up there, Granddad throws a packet of chocolate-drops up for me to eat and opens a packet himself.

'Don't tell Nana,' he says. 'I'm only meant to have chocolate twice a week.'

'I won't,' I say as my teeth clamp down and a yummy taste spreads round my mouth.

When we have our picnic, I let Granddad have
one of my crisps. He waits until Nana is watching
Theo scratch his armpit so she doesn't notice him
eating it.

'Theo, don't do that,' Nana says as Granddad's
hand **sneaks** up to his mouth. 'It's not nice for
the rest of us to look at.'

So Theo sticks his fingers in his sandwich instead
to make sure Mum put enough Marmite in. Then
he says, looking straight at Nana,

'There once was a chicken called Sue, who wanted
to go to the ...'

'Theo,' Nana says. 'Close your mouth when you chew. Otherwise your face looks like it has **dirty underwear going round in a washing machine**.' Then she says,

'What've you enjoyed doing most this morning?'

Theo says nothing while his brain tries to work and he swallows his mouthful of Marmite sandwich. Then he says,

'The acrobat on the see-saw.'

And he stands up.

And in his mind he is the acrobat and is balancing on the see-saw and he waves one arm in the air and jumps up high.

As he does, his sandwich drops on the floor.

Mum is looking for something in her bag so doesn't see Nana's **withering look** that **vaporises** the air as it travels towards him.

'Pick the sandwich up,' she says.

And while Nana is withering Theo, Ivan sneezes.

'Ivan, don't sneeze when there is food around,' Nana says and pats his head. Then in exactly the same voice she says,

'Theo, sit down or there'll be Marmite on your clothes and you'll look scruffy when I take your photograph after lunch.'

So Theo sits down, eats all his lunch, burps, licks his fingers then tidies his lunch box without saying another word. Goffo shuffles behind him, lies down and starts scratching his tummy. And scratching his tummy will make one of his fourteen-a-day pop out.

At least he is not doing it in front of Nana.

If he was, she would wither him too.

And he would ignore her.

And she would wither him again.

And he would still ignore her and it would be hilarious.

'Why don't we put Goffo and Ivan on each end of the see-saw and bounce them up and down?' Theo says when Nana is sweeping crumbs off the table with her left hand. Goffo and Ivan, hearing their names, stand up.

'Ivan, sit down,' Nana says, and Ivan's knees

71

immediately **bend like a ballerina's** and he **sinks back to planet Earth**.

'Down, Goffo,' Mum says, and Goffo rolls on to his back and waves his legs in the air.

'Victoria,' Nana says, 'if I gave you Dog Training Lessons for your birthday, would you actually take Goffo to them?'

'Probably not,' Mum sighs, pressing a headache tablet out of its silver foil and reaching for her bottle of water.

'It would make your life a lot less stressful,' Nana says. 'As Mrs Rentop said when I took Ivan, "Dogs are like people and need to know how to behave themselves".'

Next to me, Granddad mutters,

'They certainly do.'

FACT NUMBER TWENTY-THREE

At school, we line up in alphabetical order in case there is a fire and someone who doesn't know us has to take the register in a hurry. It's to do with Health and Safety.

Carl Worthington is already on a green card for belching three times during maths. He is standing behind me and we are about to walk to the hall for assembly.

'Your mum looks like a gorilla,' he whispers in my left ear.

'She doesn't,' I say.

And straight away I wish I had kept my mouth shut because he is just being mean.

And stupid.

And a bully.

And I know I must ignore him.

'Dermo's mum's a gorilla as well,' he says.

Sharon was round at our house yesterday and
Mum closed the kitchen door so we couldn't hear
anything. Dermo and I played on the PlayStation
and Theo let Dermo have some of his chocolate
bar because Dermo was upset as well. Because he
wants to see his dad and can't. So Dermo's mum
is not a gorilla. Neither is mine.

'I said, your mum and Dermo's mum are gorillas,'
Carl Worthington whispers again and I want to tell him
to shut up.

But I'm too scared to, so I say,

'They're not.'

'They are,' he says. 'That's why Dermo's dad has
gone off to Australia, because his mum scratches
her armpits all the time and has hair all over her
tummy.'

And my head freezes because no one is meant to
know that Dermo's dad has gone.

But somehow Carl Worthington knows.

And I wish I had the courage to sock him on the nose because he shouldn't be saying things like that.

Because they are horrible.

And I'm glad Mrs Logan has walked to the end of the line.

She has an orange card in her hand.

'You all right?' she says to me.

And I nod, even though I wish, every day, that we didn't have to line up in alphabetical order.

FACT NUMBER TWENTY-FOUR

There are different types of Lobelia flower. One of them is Pukewart and another is Vomitwort. Mum found those names on the internet for when we play the Visiting Game and they are brilliant.

Last week, Theo didn't line up in alphabetical order and Mr Jennings **went bananas**. Our class were first in the hall, waiting for assembly to start, when 3J came in. Theo was skipping and giggling next to Matthew Draylong.

'Theo Warren,' Mr Jennings suddenly barked, 'why are you **making a spectacle of yourself**, and why aren't you where you should be? Your surname starts with W, not D, or don't you know that yet?'

Next to me, Carl Pukewart Worthington muttered, 'Your brother is a moron.'

And I wanted to tell Carl Pukewart Worthington that Theo was probably in the wrong place because he has to sit next to Charmaine Vomitwart Worthington.

But all I did was stare at the wood blocks on the hall floor as Mr Jennings told Theo to sit next to his chair so he could **keep an eye on him**.

Today though, Theo is not in trouble because it is 3J's assembly and this could be his big break into the world of acting. 3J are doing a play and adults who are important to them turn up to watch. Mum gives me a really fast little wave as our class walk into assembly.

The play is about Robin Hood. Theo is one of the Merry Men. Mum bought some green woolly tights from a charity shop for him to wear. They are too big for Theo's skinny little legs, but he is not embarrassed about that, and mouths everyone's words when it is not his turn to speak. Mum films the whole assembly. We will watch it tonight when Dad gets home from work, sitting on the sofa, like we always do.

When 3J have finished, Miss Cortez thanks parents for coming to see the assembly and says

how amazing their children's acting has been. She
says that after every class assembly, even if it is
dead boring and the acting was rubbish. While
she speaks, Theo blows bubbles out of his mouth
and a white trail of spit slobbers down his chin
onto his chest.

I look at Mum. She has stopped filming and is
wiping her chin with her hand, hoping Theo will
see her and do the same. Only he doesn't, because
he is now busy picking his nose.

When it is 5L's turn to leave the hall, Mum is
rubbing her left eye like it has got something in
it. Matthew Draylong's mum is next to her. She
smiles at me and I smile back. The Pukewart's
mother should be here because of Charmaine. I look
along the rows but cannot see her. She must be at
work. Or the gym. Or out shopping.

Whatever was in Mum's eye seems to have gone
now because she is lifting her bag on to her lap.

She looks up at me and grins.

FACT NUMBER TWENTY-FIVE

If you divide twenty-five pounds in two equal parts, each person gets twelve pounds fifty.

Every year at school we have the **Summer Showdown** to raise money for computers, books and playground equipment. And part of the showdown is the Pet Talent Competition, and all you need for that is a pet that does daft things.

On the day, your pet has to do a trick for Rusty and Carmen, who own Purrfect Pet Shop in town. There's always another judge as well. Last year the other judge was Mrs Khan who is the school caretaker and has a rabbit called **Chicken**, a snake called **Kentucky** and a hamster called **Fried**.

The judges choose five pets for the **Final Five**, who then do their trick again with everyone watching. Carl Pukewart Worthington's cat won last year. It played a toy piano with its front paws, curled its tail round a tin of cat food and threw its head from side to side.

All at the same time.

Which was quite a clever thing to do.

And won twenty pounds for Carl Pukewart Worthington who said he spent it on a new computer game his big brother had to buy for him. He has a new cat this year, because his old one was run over, and he says he's going to enter it because the prize money has gone up to twenty-five pounds.

Anyway, it is February and the Summer Showdown is not until June, which is four months away, but Theo says he wants to enter Goffo in this year's competition.

'I'll help you as long as I get half the **prize money**,' I say.

'That's not fair,' Theo says. 'It's my idea.'

'Suit yourself,' I say, and stay in the kitchen eating a biscuit watching him trying to think of something for Goffo to do. The first thing he tries is balancing an egg on the end of Goffo's nose. It falls off and cracks on the kitchen floor, which makes me laugh until Mum tells me off for laughing and Theo off for making a mess on the kitchen floor.

We both have to clear up the mess and then Theo fetches our old tricycle from the shed to see if Goffo will sit on it.

He won't.

'If dogs were meant to sit on bicycle seats they would have been given bigger bottoms,' Mum says. 'You've got to make Goffo look like he's being clever when he's not actually doing anything.'

And as she says the word 'anything', she grabs the edge of the kitchen table and wobbles about like she's going to fall over. Then she stands up straight and takes a deep breath.

'Woooa!' she says. 'I came over all funny then.'

'Are you all right?' I say.

'Think so,' she says. 'I've got a bit of a headache and it's been a really busy day. I need some food inside me. Then I'll be fine. You two, go and find something else to do and I'll see what we're going to have for supper.'

So while she sticks sausages in the oven and peels some potatoes, Theo and I go in the back room. I have some homework to do. It's fractions and I have to concentrate really hard.

Theo has homework as well, but he goes on the PlayStation instead.

FACT NUMBER TWENTY-SIX

*If you balance a plank of wood over a
hosepipe reel, it makes a sort of see-saw.*

Mum calls out, 'Theo, can you take the tricycle
back to the shed?' But no part of Theo moves
except his thumbs.

'Theo,' Mum calls again, 'will you please take the
tricycle back to the shed.'

And suddenly an idea pops into my brain and I
don't leave it to warm up because I need to use it
straight away.

'I'll take the tricycle back to the shed for you,' I
tell him, 'as long as you give me half the prize
money if you win the competition.'

Theo still says nothing.

So I say,

'Half the prize money is mine then.'

He's not going to win anyway. I say it just to annoy him.

Goffo follows me as I walk down the garden with the tricycle and open the shed door.

In the corner, the garden hosepipe reel looks at me.

And as it does, another idea **zips out** of the **imagination box** in my brain.

I **manoeuvre** the hosepipe reel on to the grass and find one of the planks of wood Dad kept for if he ever has to repair the garden fence again.

Then I rest the plank on the hosepipe reel to make a sort of see-saw.

Mum said we must make Goffo look cleverer than he really is.

I am thinking about the Topplehurst Model Village.

And the acrobat standing on his see-saw.

All Goffo has to do is sit on the bottom of the plank.

While I walk towards the other end.

Goffo is sniffing the apple tree. I pick him up and dump him on the end of the plank resting on the ground.

'Stay, Goffo,' I say. 'Do not move.'

And sensing the **momentousness** of the occasion, and because I am wearing my **Arsenal shirt**, he wags his tail and does as he is told.

'Good boy,' I say, balancing on the middle of the plank. Then I walk towards the raised end.

It wobbles down.

Goffo's end wobbles up.

And Goffo sits there looking round, but not moving.

'Goffo,' I say, 'you are going to earn me twelve pounds fifty.'

Goffo celebrates his **launch into the entertainment world** by trotting down the plank of wood, weeing against the apple tree, then licking it clean.

I do not tell Theo about my idea for at least one hour, partly because he is **bone idle**, and partly because I want to enjoy the idea while it is still just mine.

The Pukewart always brings his football to school on Tuesdays. It's better than the school one and because it is his ball, The Pukewart also gets to pick the teams. So he chooses Marcus Smail and AJ Rivers and the other good players. And they play the rest of us. Today they score two goals before a teacher even appears on the playground. Year Threes and Fours stand watching us, wishing they could join in, which they can't because it is our day to play football.

The Pukewart **smacks** the ball straight at them. It hits Matthew Draylong's arm and bounces onto Theo's left knee. Theo suddenly bends over, grabs the ball and **shoves** it up his sweatshirt to make it

87

look like he is pregnant. He then runs up the steps towards the top playground with The Pukewart charging after him and the rest of us wondering what's going to happen next, though we sort of know already.

Dermo and I run after him, just in case.

We watch as Theo gets pulled to the ground.

But he keeps hold of the ball.

So The Pukewart starts kicking him.

'Oi,' I shout, 'leave him alone.'

But The Pukewart carries on kicking Theo and a crowd gathers round to watch and I have to do something because Theo is my little brother and I should look after him, even if he does stupid things like take The Pukewart's ball.

Although I am scared, I take a step forward and grab hold of The Pukewart's left arm.

Dermo steps forward as well and grabs his other arm.

Dermo thwacks The Pukewart in the stomach while he's at it.

And that makes The Pukewart suddenly fling both arms backwards.

I do not expect him to do that, and his left arm slips out of my hands.

The next thing I know, Dermo gets punched in the stomach.

Dermo gasps and takes a step back.

Oooofff!

And as he does, he trips over Theo's feet, throws his right arm round The Pukewart's neck and the two of them tumble to the ground.

FACT NUMBER TWENTY-EIGHT

Teachers never run on the playground because they wear high heels and have mugs of coffee in their hands. If one of them has a birthday, they have cake as well, even though cake is not a healthy dietary option or one of their five-a-day.

If there is a fight going on in the playground, teachers do not run.

But they do yell.

All teachers have loud voices they keep in their pockets for emergencies. And this is an emergency and Matthew Draylong has run to the teacher on duty.

'Carl ... Worthington,' Miss Olukajo bellows across the playground, 'leave ... that ... boy ... alone!'

By the time she arrives, The Pukewart is sitting up and pretending to cry, Dermo is gasping and holding his stomach, and Theo is still lying on the floor holding The Pukewart's football.

Miss Olukajo tells the crowd to go away.

So everyone takes one step back as two **responsible** Year Sixes are chosen to take Carl Worthington straight to Miss Cortez's office.

'He started it,' The Pukewart shouts, pointing at Theo. 'He took my football.'

'After you deliberately kicked it at him,' I say.

'I didn't,' he shouts.

'You did,' I yell back.

'They're always blaming me,' The Pukewart says.

'Because you're the one who starts everything,' Dermo joins in.

'Miss Cortez can deal with all of you,' Miss Olukajo says. She turns to me and Dermo and Theo.

'You three can go and see Miss Cortez as well.'

'But he was kicking me,' Theo starts.

'You can tell that to Miss Cortez,' she says and asks two more responsible Year Sixes to take us to the nurse to make sure we are not injured.

Then we must go to Miss Cortez's office.

FACT NUMBER TWENTY-NINE

I have only ever had three green cards before.

Miss Cortez's **nostrils flare outwards** as she hands us orange cards and opens the folder where the orange card sheets are kept. We then sit at the tables in her office and write about what we will do next time we feel angry. I want to write that if The Pukewart stopped coming to our school, I wouldn't feel angry.

But I don't.

Instead I write that I will count to ten or tell the teacher.

When we have finished filling in our sheets, which she will now keep as evidence, Miss Cortez tells us again how disappointed she is with our behaviour and sends me, Dermo and Theo back to our classrooms.

'And you, Carl ... can stay here,' she says.

'You all right where he kicked you?' I ask Theo once we're outside her office. He isn't standing up straight when he walks.

'No,' he says. 'It hurts.'

'What are we going to tell Mum?' I say. 'She'll have a **hissy fit** if she thinks we've been fighting.'

'We haven't been fighting,' Theo says. 'He attacked me.'

'Yeah. Cos you were a numbskull and ran off with his ball,' Dermo says.

'After he kicked it straight at me,' Theo says.

And I say,

'I've never had an orange card before.'

'Haven't you?' Theo says.

'No, I haven't.'

'Nor me,' Dermo says.

And Theo looks at us like we're from a different planet.

'I get them all the time,' he says.

'What? Mr Jennings gives you orange cards?'

'Yeah.'

'What for?' I ask.

Theo wrinkles his mouth towards his nose so his front teeth show. Then he says,

'Burping, belching, chewing gum, cutting peoples' hair, throwing rubbers. Last one was for putting snow down Charmaine Worthington's back.'

'You ever had a red card?' Dermo asks.

'I'm not that stupid,' Theo says.

FACT NUMBER THIRTY

Dermo's dad was meant to Skype him before school this morning. Only he didn't.

5L is four doors down the corridor from 3J.

'I don't want my mum to know I've got an orange card either,' Dermo says when Theo has gone into his classroom. 'Promise, promise, promise not to say a word.'

'Promise will be kept,' I say in a robot voice.

Everyone looks up when we walk through the door.

'Sit down,' Mrs Logan says. 'I'm really surprised at you two. I thought you knew better than to fight.'

She does not smile.

But Skye and Alice do.

Dermo's shoulder is hurting.

He rests his left elbow on the table and pulls a face.

We are doing page forty-five in our maths books.

'Section B,' Skye whispers.

Dermo's pencil needs sharpening. He opens his pencil case, but his sharpener isn't there.

He asks if he can borrow mine.

Mine's gone missing too.

'Carl used my sharpener before playtime,' Alice whispers and looks at the bulging pencil case lying on his table. 'I bet it's in there.'

It's **verging on dangerous** to touch any of The Pukowart's things. Only today, Dermo doesn't care. He picks up the pencil case and quickly undoes the zip. Skye lifts her maths book up so AJ won't be able to see what Dermo's doing and **snitch**. Alice's eyes follow Mrs Logan to make sure she doesn't come over and I watch the door. It is like we all know what to do without anyone telling us.

'Here's my sharpener,' Dermo whispers, taking it out. 'And Alice's. And here's your rubber,' he says to me.

'And here's your ruler,' he says to Skye. 'And Alice's key ring.'

'He'll know we've been in his pencil case,' I whisper.

And we all look at each other.

And I am thinking, 'Is it worth it?'

But Dermo says,

'We're just getting back what's ours.' Then he says. 'I'm sick of him.'

So am I.

But I'm scared of him as well.

I hated what happened in the playground.

Mum and Dad say fighting is always wrong.

Dermo is putting the pencil case back when I wonder if my old whiteboard pen is in The Pukewart's pencil case as well. So I reach my hand out and take it. The zip opens easily. And there is a pen that is just like my old one.

Do I take it?

The Pukewart will do something to get back at us. The door handle suddenly turns.

'Quick,' Dermo says and I take the pen and put the pencil case back. Skye's maths book returns to a flat position on the table. We all slip what's ours in our own cases and turn our heads, like everyone else, to watch The Pukewart walk across the classroom.

'We're on page forty-five,' Mrs Logan says to him. 'Sit down and get on with it.'

He scowls at me and Dermo and throws himself in his seat.

I don't like the look on his face.

'Hate your wimpy little brother,' he says. 'He started it.'

And actually, Carl is sort of right. And I hate it that he's sort of right.

The silver Peugeot arrives first. Goffo is already
in the garden. Elise has two huge Easter eggs in
her bag.

'Thank you,' Theo and I say as we give her
high-fives.

She has something else in her bag as well.

'I thought about you when I was making these,'
she says, and takes out two pencil sharpeners.
'They are **prototypes*** and they are the only ones
in the whole world.'

---

*Prototypes are what designers make to see if what they are making is
going to work.

Theo looks at his **dinosaur pencil sharpener**. It has a long green neck, a tiny head and stomping feet.

I look at mine.

It is just like Goffo.

'That's brilliant!' I say.

And we both say, 'Thank you,' again.

And we really mean it.

'You can keep them,' Elise says. 'But they're not the **finished product**. I'm still working on that.'

'What else are you going to do to them?' Dad asks.

'Not telling,' she says. 'You'll have to wait.'

Last week, Dermo and I went on a football course and everyone was given a certificate. Mine said I had improved in **dribbling and shooting**. I go upstairs to fetch it to show Elise and Grandpa.

While I am up there, Chrissie arrives.

'Has your headache cleared?' she asks Mum as she takes her coat off.

'It's a bit better,' Mum says and then asks Chrissie what time Natters is arriving. She was with her dad last night and he's dropping her off later today.

I take my certificate downstairs and as I am showing Elise, Goffo starts barking in the garden and Theo shouts,

'Fffffourteen!' and Elise looks at Theo, then at me, and smiles.

I think she has **twigged** why we shout fffffourteen.

But because she is an adult, she is pretending she hasn't.

This year, Theo sent an e-mail telling everyone what he wanted for his birthday.

Nana and Granddad are late because there was an accident on the motorway. But they are safely here now and Mum is clearing the empty mugs away before Theo opens his presents. As she does, she drops Grandpa's mug and he has left a bit of coffee in the bottom and it runs over my football certificate. Nana takes my certificate to the kitchen to dry it and I go with her.

'That's the second time your mum has dropped something today,' Nana says to me. 'I think she is overdoing it and needs a holiday because she's not usually clumsy, is she?' And I shake my head because she's not.

And then it is time for Theo to open his presents.

He does well and remembers to say, 'Thank you,' and give **hugs of gratitude** to all the right people, until there is just one present left.

It is a small present covered in dinosaur wrapping paper.

From Chrissie and Natters.

He freezes, **glaring** at it.

'Aren't you going to open it?' Mum says.

Theo does not move.

Ivan shifts his bottom two centimetres towards Nana's right shoe.

Nana lowers her hand and pats his head.

'What's up, Theo?' Mum says.

'I wanted a tarantula,' he whispers, 'in a tank. And that present is not a tank.'

The adults **swivel** their eyes so they can look at each other without turning their heads. 'I sent e-mails asking for one,' he carries on.

He did, and it said . . .

Dear Everyone,

for my birthday I would like a twin brother called Otto and a tarantula spider in a tank.

I am having a party with a dinosaur cake.

from

Theo Warren.

'I sent an e-mail,' he says again, his voice winding up, and he walks slowly over to Mum and buries his head in her shoulder and starts crying.

'Theo,' Dad says, and I can tell he is cross, 'you've had so many lovely presents. You've got an all-singing, all-dancing waterproof watch . . .'

'I am never ever going to wear that stupid watch,' Theo screams.

'And you, young man,' Dad says, 'can just apologise to Elise and Grandpa who spent ages choosing it for you.'

'I wanted a tarantula!' Theo screams.

'I want never gets,' Nana says in her scary teacher's voice. And it's like every adult in the room is turning on him.

'Well it should get!' Theo explodes and Nana's **eyes nearly shoot out of the top of her head**. Even Ivan crosses his front paws to show his disgust. No one talks to Nana like that, or they end up with a star chart to make them behave themselves.

'Theo, look at me,' Mum says calmly. 'I can't be doing with this. Say sorry to Elise and Grandpa, then open your last present. It's from Chrissie and Natters.'

'Don't want it,' Theo shouts. 'It stinks.'

'Theo,' Mum says again, 'say sorry and open your present.'

And now Theo has everyone on the edge of their seats, he whispers, 'Sorry,' which he doesn't mean, and everyone starts **breathing normally** again as he lets out a last little sob and climbs on to Mum's lap.

Chrissie gives Theo a dinosaur card game and a whoopee cushion, which he is too weak to blow up.

Theo tries to blow the whoopee cushion up, but can't.

So I take it from him, blow it up, put it on the floor and tell him to sit on it.

There is a long low rumble.

Even Nana smiles.

A little bit.

Ivan's nose waves in the air, just for a second.

Then he shifts his body backwards, about one centimetre.

'But you **gobbed** on it,' Theo shouts at me. 'It was my present, and you took it off me.'

'Because you were too weak to blow it up,' I say back to him.

Adult eyes swivel towards me.

No one is laughing any more.

And because it's Theo's birthday and because it's what Mum and Dad would want me to do, I take the whoopee cushion to the kitchen and turn on the tap so everyone can hear it running.

I stick the cushion under the tap to make it wet then lick the mouthpiece with as much spit as I can make in three seconds, which isn't that much. Then I return to the front room.

And everyone is smiling again.

FACT NUMBER THIRTY-FOUR

The square on the calendar for yesterday read Theo swimming with Matthew. *Today's square has* DREW 12.30 *written on it in red pen.*

Last week, Mum went to the opticians, Dad went to **Ottawa**, the capital city of Canada, I went to Dermo's for a sleepover and Theo went to a pizza party.

Today is Tuesday. We lose the playtime Year Five football match by seven goals to nil. But The Pukewart is in a good mood because of it, so the day is OK. He has never said anything about us having our own rulers and sharpeners and pens back, though he must know we went in his pencil case.

I keep wondering what he will do to get his own back.

But he has done nothing yet.

Chrissie collects me and Theo from school. She says Mum's been held up in Sarrington. Goffo jumps all over us when we open the back door, then dives into the garden to say hello to the apple trees. Chrissie puts her pink laptop on the kitchen table and opens it up.

'Who's Drew?' I ask.

'Drew?' Chrissie says.

'Drew. Who Mum's gone to see. It's on the calendar.'

'Oh,' Chrissie says, 'a friend she was at school with. Hasn't seen for ages. They met up for lunch and now she's stuck in roadworks. She won't be long.'

I go in the back room to watch television.

Goffo comes in from the garden and lies across my tummy.

Theo is on the PlayStation in the corner.

He is humming so he must be winning.

After a while, Natters arrives. Her best friend, Janine, lives two roads away from our house and they walk home together. I roll off the sofa and head for the kitchen to find something to eat and see what Natters is doing.

Goffo comes with me.

'You know you want to win the Pet Talent Competition because that boy on your table's entering his cat and you want to beat him?' Natters says.

And I nod.

I so want to beat Carl.

'Well I've had an idea,' Natters says. 'When you have Goffo at the top of the plank, why doesn't Theo hold a tray next to him like he is a waiter so Goffo can walk onto it. Theo could then walk round with him on the tray.'

'I like that idea,' Chrissie says, looking over the top of her laptop.

But Goffo has **no intention whatsoever** of standing on a tray, until we **bribe** him, with a pig's ear.

Then he will do anything.

'Stay,' Natters says, and he does.

Natters gently lifts the tray with Goffo on it off the ground.

Goffo still doesn't move, except for his eyes.

They get wider and wider, the higher he goes.

'Good boy. Stay,' I say.

'Stay,' Natters says.

'Stay,' Chrissie joins in.

Then we all say 'stay' together.

And he does.

He is level with our eyes, **perched** on the tray.

We have never seen him so still.

He is like Ivan after Nana has barked at him and he is withered.

'You know what?' Chrissie says. 'He's terrified.'

'You know what,' Natters says, 'I think you are right.'

'You know what,' I say, 'he looks hilarious.'

Because he does.

'Theo has got to do it in the competition,' Natters says as she lowers the tray back down.

When Mum comes home, Theo and Natters and I are all in the back room. Dad's briefcase thumps on the hall carpet as the front door closes.

He's home early.

And at the same time as Mum.

Mum's shoes walk straight to the kitchen.

Dad sticks his head round the door to see if we are all right, which we are because not much can go wrong when you are watching the television, playing on the PlayStation or doing homework.

Then he follows Mum into the kitchen and closes the door behind him so we can't hear what they are saying.

A few minutes later I stand up.

'You're not going to the kitchen, are you?' Natters says.

'I'm going to do a poo if you must know,' I say back.

'That's all right then,' Natters says. 'You must not go in the kitchen.'

'Why not?' Theo says.

'Because the grown-ups are in there and have shut the door. That means they want to be left in peace.'

I only do a wee, but I don't tell Natters.

She thinks I do a poo, but I know I didn't.

And she doesn't know I didn't.

So I am the winner.

FACT NUMBER THIRTY-FIVE

Drawing circles with tomato ketchup is easy.

A few minutes later, the kitchen door opens. I stand up to go and see Mum.

'Don't go out,' Natters says.

'Why?'

'Just don't.' And the way she says it makes me think she knows something I don't. I am about to ask her what, when Dad comes in and says,

'Mum's got one of her headaches so is going to lie down, and Chrissie's cooking supper.'

'OK,' Natters says, like she knew Dad was going to say that.

'What's up?' I ask her as Dad goes back to the kitchen.

'Nothing,' Natters says straight away.

Which means there is.

And all I can think is,

I wish Mum didn't have these headaches.

Chrissie makes shepherd's pie. We sit round the kitchen table as she drains carrots into Mum's sieve and Natters tells Dad about the idea she's had for Goffo's trick using a tray.

'But I don't want a tray,' Theo says as Chrissie puts plates of food in front of us. 'It was my idea to enter the competition and you're changing everything.'

His voice is winding up and it's going to be one of those wind-ups when only Mum can get him to shut up.

Only she's not here.

She's upstairs with a headache.

'Theo,' Dad says, 'we'll sort the trick out later when you aren't so tired.'

'I'm not tired,' he wails. 'And I'm not eating this either. It looks like dog poo with seagull poo on top and it stinks.'

Chrissie ignores him and squirts a **dollop** of tomato ketchup on the side of her plate. I take the bottle next and draw a red circle on top of the potato. The last circle I drew was over macaroni cheese and it went all **squiffy** because the bottle was nearly empty and the sauce **splattered** out and sounded like it was passing wind. Today's circle is a perfect one. And while I am drawing it, Dad says very calmly and very quietly,

'Theo, you are not going to talk to Chrissie like that. Say you are sorry.'

Natters scoops food on to her fork and sticks it in her mouth.

I do the same.

The shepherd's pie tastes OK.

But Theo has crawled on to Dad's lap and Dad is rocking him and feeding him like a baby and calling him 'Little Chicken', which is not fair because Theo has not said 'sorry' to Chrissie.

And no one says anything because Dad has tears in his eyes and is pushing the shepherd's pie round his plate with his fork.

In the corner, Goffo finishes scratching himself and does an enormous blow-off. But no one giggles or laughs or whispers fourteen or even looks at anyone else.

Because something has happened.

And I don't know what it is.

My coat is lying on the floor.

I pick it up.

Someone has emptied my PE bag and stamped on my T-shirt and shorts.

And now there are muddy footprints all over them.

Tears prick the back of my eyes, but I am not going to cry because AJ's shoes are next to my PE bag.

He is putting his coat on.

So I keep my head bent over and my fingers wrap round my T-shirt and I am shoving it back inside the bag when Dermo crouches on the floor next to me.

His eyes look at mine. Then he turns and stands up, like he is protecting me, and I stay behind the back of his legs because a tear is now rolling down my cheek. And it's rolling because a pathetic, stupid bully emptied my PE things on to the floor.

He didn't punch me.

Or kick me.

He hasn't said anything nasty.

He didn't take anything from me either.

I stay there until AJ's shoes join the The Pukewart's luminous green laces as they leave the cloakroom.

And I can hear them sniggering as they go.

'I'm going to tell Mrs Logan,' Dermo says.

'No, it's all right,' I say.

'It's not all right,' he says. 'You don't need them bullying you. Not now. Come on.'

And he grabs the PE bag out of my hands.

'We're going to tell her,' he says.

Mrs Logan is sorting out things for her art club. Charmaine Vomitwart Worthington and her friend, Princess Fielding, are helping.

'Mrs Logan,' Dermo says, holding up the muddy bag, 'George's PE bag's been emptied on the floor and trodden on.'

'Are you sure your PE bag was on your peg?' Mrs Logan asks.

And I nod and wipe my cheek with the back of my hand and wish I could tell the tears to go away.

Mrs Logan sighs.

'I thought things had been better recently,' she says.

And they have.

Since the fight in the playground, The Pukewart's been OK. We've stuck together, and he's backed off.

'It's horrible,' Mrs Logan says. 'But I think the best thing is to leave your PE bag on my table and I'll deal with it in the morning.'

Mrs Logan's face is a frown and a smile and a sadness, all rolled into one. She puts her arm round my shoulder and says,

'I will get this sorted because I am here to look after you and I won't have bullying in my classroom.'

And all I can think is that Charmaine Vomitwart Worthington will tell The Pukewart I was crying.

And if he knows, he has won.

And I have lost.

Mrs Logan tells Princess Fielding and The Vomitwart to go and find some paint under the sink on the other side of the classroom.

'I want to sit on another table,' I whisper.

'And me,' Dermo says. 'Can we move?'

'I'll have a think about that one,' Mrs Logan says.

Best friends stand up for you.

I put my coat on and do up the zip.

Then we walk across the playground together.

'My dad's Skyping me tonight,' Dermo says.
'Wish I could go out and see him. Then I could
miss some school.'

And my heart skips a beat because I don't want
Dermo to go. I want him to always be in school.
Because he's my best friend and because if he
wasn't here, I know The Pukewart would be much
more horrible to me.

Outside the gate, Theo is standing next to Sharon
holding a model shield he made out of a cardboard
box. He brought it in to show Mr Jennings.

'Hello,' Sharon says. 'You two are late. Is everything all right?'

And we both nod, even though it isn't.

Goffo is in his cage which is on the front seat of her car. He's been to Squire Woods so is still excited because he's been talking to the rabbits. Dermo, Theo and I strap ourselves in the back.

'Ffffourteen,' Theo says for no reason.

But I'm not in the mood to giggle or listen to him, so I ignore him.

'What's up with you then?' he says.

'Nothing,' I say. 'Just shut up.'

Because I want the world to go away.

It is 4.17 in the morning and I have just woken up.

Mum says if I wear cotton socks my feet won't sweat so much.

Then they might stop itching.

So Dad buys me some cotton socks at the supermarket.

But they're lying on the floor because they are dirty.

And I can't be bothered to put them in the linen basket.

Henry Snail has gone to sniff them out.

Well I hope he has, because I can't find him under my quilt.

I lean out of bed and run my hand over my Arsenal rug until I find him. Granddad and Nana gave Henry Snail to me when Theo was born.

I loved snails then.

I still do.

Henry Snail is now between my left elbow and my rib cage. He wants to go to sleep but can't because my right foot is itching.

There is a piece of **flaky** skin underneath my big toe, like a little flap. I scratch it until the flap gets really long. Then it peels off altogether.

And for a second the itch actually does stop itching.

Then it starts all over again.

And I hate being awake in the middle of the night because it is so boring.

But it does give me time to think.

And I do have a lot to think about because things have suddenly changed.

1. The Pukewart has been moved to another table. And that is brilliant.

2. Theo and I stayed with Sharon and Dermo last week because Mum went to hospital so doctors could find out why she keeps having headaches. She's back home now with a bandage round her head that makes her look like **Mr Bump**. But the doctors have given her pills to make her better, so she is going to be all right.

3. Chrissie collects me and Theo from school. She used to do that a bit before, but now it's nearly every day. And if Chrissie can't be there, Sharon brings us home.

4. Mum does not tell funny stories about what she has been doing like she used to. She's often in bed or in the back room resting her head on a cushion and Dad has asked us to be extra quiet and extra good to help Mum get better.

5. Sharon takes Goffo to Squire Wood for Mum. Dad takes him to the park. So do I sometimes, which must be very boring for him because he likes chasing rabbits.

6. Mrs Shardini buys things if Dad gets the internet order wrong. She buys us **yummy chocolate biscuits**, Hawaiian and pepperoni pizzas and **red pepper humus**. Mrs Shardini has stopped going swimming as well. At least, her

pink bikini and her towel are not on the washing line every Wednesday like they used to be. Theo thinks she has taken up **sumo wrestling** instead and started a new poem about her. He got stuck on the last line so I finished it for him.

There once was a lady next door,
Whose tummy came down to the floor.
She **sumoed** away,
For many a day,
And then started wrestling some more.

7. Dad comes home earlier from work and helps with the cooking. He is rubbish at cooking. Chrissie is trying to help him get better. Sometimes he works at home all day. Dad does the washing and ironing as well. He **burped** really loudly three times last Saturday as he folded Theo's school sweatshirt. Only he didn't giggle like he would have done a few months ago.

8. Mum and I still play Scrabble. We played yesterday and I won only I don't think she was trying, so I didn't really win.

9. Theo has started waking up in the night. I can hear him now. He is mumbling to himself. He

could be taking his pyjamas off or making a
den in the corner of his bedroom.

Or he could be about to take his quilt and pillow
on to the landing like he did last night.

I stare at my curtains waiting for Theo's bedroom door to open. If it does, I will go out and tell him to go back to bed. If Theo's door doesn't open, I'll try and go back to sleep.

And then Theo's door handle clicks. My feet swing towards the Arsenal cannon. Theo mustn't reach the loose floorboard outside the bathroom or it will bang and Dad will wake up. I don't want Dad to wake up because Chrissie says he needs a good night's sleep.

Theo is only wearing his pyjama bottoms. Gregory Grasshopper is tucked under his right

131

arm. He is standing completely still, like he doesn't know what to do next.

I tiptoe towards him and turn him round.

'Little Chicken, back to bed,' I whisper, which is what Dad always says. And as Dad is the only person who ever calls him Little Chicken, I **reckon** Theo will think I'm Dad and do what I tell him.

Theo's pyjama top is on the floor.

I pick it up.

'Little Chicken, put this back on,' I whisper, handing it to him. He does exactly as I tell him and shoves his hands and arms inside it.

'Little Chicken, get back into bed,' I hiss, and he climbs on his mattress and lies there cuddling Gregory Grasshopper.

'Little Chicken, you are a pain in the neck. If you get out of bed and wake me up again, I'll pour a bucket of cold water over your head and take Gregory Grasshopper to a zoo. Got it? Now go back to sleep.'

And I drop the quilt over him.

I never hear what Dad says after he's taken Theo back to bed. I only ever hear the landing bit.

But telling Theo to stay in bed seems a sensible sort of thing to do.

FACT NUMBER FORTY

Everyone smiles and tries to look happy in photographs.

Chrissie and Mum decide we can have a barbecue after school and each of us can invite a friend.

So Theo invites Matthew Draylong and Natters invites Janine.

And here's another thing that is different.

Lots of people have keys to our house.

Sharon has one.

So does Chrissie.

So does Mrs Shardini.

They all know the burglar alarm number.

0628.

And they do because they are helping Mum get better.

We wake her up to tell her we are home. A magazine is lying on her lap. It is open at a page with a picture of a giraffe wearing a long scarf that is an advert for sore throat **lozenges**. The giraffe is female because she has hair between her ears. Male giraffes are bald.

Sharon has some doughnuts.

'I bet you can't eat these without licking your lips,' she says.

She is right, we can't, even though we try.

Chrissie arrives a few minutes later with Natters and Janine who giggle at each other because they have female **hormones** that make them feel embarrassed. They go to Theo's bedroom to change out of their school uniforms while Chrissie writes out exactly what time and for how long each of us can go on the PlayStation, trampoline or be in charge of the television. We will **rotate** round and not **squabble** or argue.

Chrissie has twenty-four bread rolls in a resealable pack, pasta salad, coleslaw, a huge packet of crisps, a **guacamole** dip and vanilla ice cream with chocolate sauce.

'It's to celebrate the first barbecue of the summer,' she says.

Sharon and Mum sit on reclining chairs with their feet up.

Dad has been working at home today and he sits next to Matthew Draylong who writes the initials of his name on his plate in tomato ketchup. Theo then spills his lemonade, but it doesn't matter because we are outside.

Janine tells stupid jokes that aren't funny. But everyone laughs and passes food to each other and we are just enjoying ourselves and Theo and Matthew Draylong make up a limerick and it is so stupid, Dermo and I get the giggles.

> A barbecue sat on the loo,
> Because it was doing a poo.
> And while it did,
> A man called Sid,
> Made sausages go blue.'

And then everyone starts making up limericks until Theo says,

'A man called Number Fourteen.' And Mum says,

'Theo, please do not do your ridiculous fourteen thing.' And as she says 'thing', a wasp lands on the table and Janine screams. So Dad traps the wasp under a glass and it keeps hitting its head trying to escape and Chrissie takes photographs of us pulling silly faces at the wasp.

And we are all laughing.

Because it is brilliant, like before Mum started getting headaches.

Like before all the different things started happening.

And Dermo and I sit next to each other and finish our first lot of ice cream then have some more.

FACT NUMBER FORTY-ONE

People with cancer *wear headscarves and everyone gets excited when they raise money for charity.*

Dermo and I have our turn on the trampoline after we have finished eating. We jump extra high for eighty-four jumps then sit down to get our breaths back and let our food settle.

'My mum says your mum's probably got cancer,' Dermo says in a quiet voice that is more like a whisper. 'Has she?'

The words make me freeze.

'No,' I say. 'She has a headache that won't go away and makes her feel tired. The doctor's given her medicine and she's getting better.'

But Dermo carries on.

'When you and Theo stayed with us, did your mum see a brain doctor or a cancer doctor?'

The safety net round the trampoline is tall and it's dark, and when I whisper,

'I don't know,' my voice seems very little. And Dermo is looking like he's thinking he should have kept his mouth shut.

'You know that calendar on your kitchen wall,' he suddenly says. 'We could see if there are doctor's appointments on it and a doctor's name.'

All I can think is,

I don't want to.

And then I think,

'If Mum has got cancer, why haven't they told me and Theo?'

'Come on,' Dermo says and his feet are already over the side of the trampoline. 'Let's look on the calendar. Maybe she hasn't.'

And I don't want to go, but I force my legs to follow him.

Chrissie and Dad are still at the table talking to Mum and Sharon about going on holiday with Nana and Granddad, like we did last year.

'You all right?' Chrissie says as we walk past them.

'Just going to the loo,' Dermo says.

We go through the back door and into the kitchen.

'Here's the calendar,' I whisper, lifting it off its hook.

'Who's DREW?' Dermo asks, pointing to the word.

'Chrissie said she was Mum's friend.'

'Have you ever met her?'

I shake my head.

'Your mum's seeing her again on May the eleventh. That's next week,' he whispers and flicks through the rest of the calendar. I want him to stop because I want to go back to when we were all laughing at Janine's stupid jokes and the wasp inside the glass and making up limericks.

But I know that's never going to happen.

'Your mum was out loads in January and February and March,' he whispers.

'But there's nothing for her this month. Except DREW.'

And I feel trembly all over. It's like ... I don't know what it's like, but it's ...

'Which hospital has she been going to?' he asks.

'Chrissie said DREW lived in Sarrington,' I say.

Or was that something Chrissie made up?

'There is a hospital at Sarrington,' Dermo whispers.

'And that's where she went when Theo and I stayed with you,' I whisper back.

'Right. Let's see if a Doctor DREW works there. We need a computer.'

'Dad's old laptop's in my bedroom,' I say.

And my voice is very quiet.

'You do it,' I tell Dermo.

I'm really, really scared.

Please, DREW, don't be a doctor.

Dermo opens up Google and types in 'Sarrington Hospital'. The hospital website says it has five-hundred-and-seventy-eight beds and two-hundred-and-ninety-four parking spaces.

It also has a guide to its doctors.

None of them are called DREW.

I smile inside, just a little bit.

Maybe Dermo's got it wrong.

Until he says,

'D R is short for doctor, isn't it?'

And my heart bangs so fast as Dermo tries again and types in 'Dr EW' and presses ENTER.

'Dr Erin Winter, head of Oncology Department' appears on the screen.

'There's DREW,' Dermo says. 'Doctor Erin Winter.'

'But she's not a cancer doctor,' I say. 'She's onc . . . onc . . . ology, whatever that is.'

Then Dermo says slowly in a totally flat voice,

'George, oncology means cancer.' And he'll know that because his granddad died of cancer last year. But Mum and I have never played the Visiting Game with hospital words.

So I don't know what oncology means.

And all I can whisper is,

'No it doesn't.'

And Dermo just looks at me.

'It does,' he whispers.

And all I can say is,

'Why haven't Mum and Dad told me?'

And all he says is,

'I found out because I heard my mum talking to your mum on the phone. And I'm not meant to have told you. Promise, promise, promise you won't say anything.'

'Promise will be kept,' I say.

But I cannot get my voice to sound like a robot.

When I asked Chrissie who DREW was, she said Mum had gone to visit a friend.

But she told me a lie because it wasn't a friend.

It was Doctor Erin Winter, at Sarrington Hospital.

Who is a cancer doctor.

And Dad pretended he had come home early from work that day and fed Theo like he was a baby and called him Little Chicken.

But Dad had been to Sarrington Hospital.

With Mum.

And that day, Natters knew what was going on, because she told me not to go in the kitchen when I said I was going to the loo.

And Mrs Shardini knows because she lives next door and does bits of shopping for us.

And Nana and Granddad know because they go in the kitchen and shut the door.

And Grandpa and Elise know, because last Saturday Elise took us to the park and Theo wanted to go back home. But Elise said she wanted to play football for a while longer. So we did. And that was a lie because she didn't really want to play football but while we were there, Grandpa and Mum and Dad were at home, talking.

And Sharon knows because she collects us from school and takes Goffo to Squire Woods to chase rabbits.

And everyone being happy at the barbecue tonight was a lie too, like pretending everything is OK.

When it isn't.

But Dermo told me the truth, because he is my **best friend** and we promise, promise, promise. And then I think about the time The Pukewart trod muddy footprints all over my PE things and how Dermo said – and the words are **crystal clear** in my mind because they didn't quite make sense – he said, 'You don't need them bullying you. Not now.'

'How long have you known?' I ask him.

'About three weeks,' he whispers and he is looking straight at me.

He knew.

'Do you think Mrs Logan knows?' I whisper.

'Dunno,' he says. 'She moved Carl to another table, so maybe she does.'

And suddenly I think about Theo.

Because I don't think he knows about Mum either.

And even though he is in Year Three and still learning to grow up, **he is my brother**.

Henry Snail's tummy is hurting because he wants the dark thoughts *to go away.*

My eyes are closed.

I am too scared to open them.

Because dark thoughts have moved into my brain.

It feels like they are taking over.

They make me feel like I am all alone.

Even though I know I'm not.

They make me feel as if everyone else is having a lovely time.

And smiling.

But I don't want to join in.

Because all I can think about is Mum.

And what is going to happen.

> ## FACT NUMBER FORTY-FIVE
>
> *When I forget about the* dark thoughts *I can pretend that everything is all right.*

But then the dark thoughts always come back.

And when they do, they are always a little bit bigger than they were before.

But I don't tell anyone about them.

Because I am not supposed to know.

About Mum.

Only I do.

'You all right?' Dermo says.

'Yup,' I say.

And he knows I'm not.

We are doing persuasive writing in literacy and have to write a letter to the council telling them to let Little Red Riding Hood's grannie live in a retirement home. Being in the woods is no longer a **viable option** because the wolf family are **terrorising** her and the woodcutter has put his back out protecting her.

We have to write another persuasive letter for our homework. This one is from the three bears, asking Goldilocks's parents to repair their house.

Chrissie reads it after I have finished and laughs out loud.

'You're so good with words,' she says. 'Go and read it to your mum.'

So I go in the back room and Mum thinks my homework is funny as well.

And all the time I am looking at her.

And I know what is in her head.

And I know why she is tired all the time.

And why she doesn't talk so much.

Or go out unless someone is with her.

And I want to ask her about it.

I want to tell her I know.

But I can't.

Because I promise, promise, promised I wouldn't say anything.

She asks me to fetch a glass of water for her.

And when I bring it back I put it on a coaster on the coffee table, which used to be in the front room but now lives in the back because it is the right height for Mum to put her things on.

And she smiles and says,

'Thank you.'

And as she does, the dark thoughts stretch their fingers and squeeze my brain.

Mum hears Theo read. Yesterday he moved up to buff colour reading books so his new book has fewer pictures and harder words in. She signs his home-school book to say he has read up to page sixteen.

Chrissie signed Theo's home-school book two weeks ago.

Chrissie Cooper.

Dad signed last week.

Jack Warren.

Mum signs it this week.

Vicky Warren.

Theo says he wants a different person to sign his book each week, so I am going to sign it next with my neatest signature, and Natters is going to do it the week after that.

We have chicken curry for supper. I love chicken curry, but today it goes round and round my mouth and I can't swallow it.

'You all right?' Mum says.

'I'm fine,' I say.

And she knows I'm not really.

But she doesn't ask me again.

Because she is too tired.

'I bought a packet of sunflower seeds today,' Chrissie says as she chops up an apple and banana to go with chocolate ice cream. 'And a bag of compost. I thought we could plant one seed for everyone in our family and see whose grows the biggest. It'll be like a competition.'

Mum watches through the patio doors as Theo and I put compost in little pots. Natters is in

the kitchen. She has a load of homework
to do.

'We need to do one for Theo and George and
your mum and your dad and Nana and Granddad
and Elise and Grandpa and Goffo and Ivan and
Natters and me,' Chrissie says. 'That's twelve, isn't
it?'

'We could do one for Janine as well,' I say.

'You fancy her, don't you,' Theo says.

'I do not,' I say.

'Janine, Janine, where have you been? You've
been to London to visit the queen,' he chants.
'I'm telling Natters!'

'No you're not, you little poo-faced alien,' I shout
at him.

'I'm definitely telling Natters,' Theo says and he
points his finger at me and starts laughing.

'Woah,' Chrissie says. 'Both of you, stop.'

'But I don't fancy her and he's going on and on
about it,' I say.

'Theo,' Chrissie says, 'I never want to hear you repeat what you just said.'

And all Theo does is stick his tongue out at me and pull a stupid face.

We plant the seeds and Chrissie writes everyone's
names on little plastic sticks, one for each pot,
and says what a fun thing this is to do. Theo spills
compost all over the patio and Chrissie says it
doesn't matter and she'll clear it up after we've
finished.

'If we do another two pots, there will be
fffffourteen,' Theo says. But I don't find him
funny.

When the seeds are all planted, we bring the pots
indoors and line them up on the kitchen window
sill. Then Chrissie wants to know how the trick
with Goffo is getting on.

'Why don't we get the hosepipe reel and plank out and see if we can add anything else to it?' she says. 'Your mum can watch through the patio window and see what we're doing.'

I don't really want to because I know Chrissie is trying to do things with us so we don't find out about Mum.

I don't want to be cheerful either. And my head is so tired. It's like the dark thoughts are hatching eggs that burst into little creepy-crawlies that burrow through every part of my brain. But I have to keep going like they aren't there and like I don't know.

Chrissie opens the shed and Theo helps her pull the hose reel and plank up to the top of the garden. Natters is fed up doing homework so joins us. And Goffo, who thinks he is on for a pig's ear, wags his tail and sniffs the plank.

'Shall I fetch the big tray or the little one?' Natters says.

'Big one,' Chrissie says.

'He won't do it,' Theo says.

158

'Be fun to try though,' Chrissie says.

'I don't want to,' Theo says. 'The competition was my idea and you're all changing it.'

'We're not so much changing it as helping you win,' Chrissie says. 'Let's try the tray and see if it works. It'll turn the trick into a **proper performance** and the judges will love it and you are more likely to win the prize.'

Theo can still taste chicken curry. It has the same effect as when he can still taste Hawaiian pizza.

It makes him **compliant.***

So Natters fetches the big tray from the kitchen and gives it to Theo who stands at the lower end of the plank, next to where Goffo is sitting waiting to be wobbled up.

'Good boy. Stay ... ' I say to him from the middle of the plank.

Then I slowly walk towards the raised end.

It wobbles down.

The other end wobbles up.

---

*We had the word 'compliant' in our morning work last week. It means you agree to do something.

And Goffo wobbles up with it.

Theo holds the tray next to where the plank stops going up.

Goffo doesn't know whether to slide down the plank or go on the tray.

'Come on,' Theo says. 'You can do it, Goffo.'

And Goffo does and his feet slide onto the tray and his legs **quiver** as he steadies himself.

'Stay,' Theo says.

And Goffo does.

Chrissie and Natters laugh and clap. Mum has been watching from the back room and she is slowly clapping as well.

'Theo, if you are a waiter,' Chrissie says, 'why don't we dress you up with a bowtie and black jacket?'

And Theo smiles because he loves dressing up because then everyone looks at him.

Goffo stands **absolutely** still on the tray.

'Theo, walk round the see-saw with the tray held up high,' Natters says.

And Theo does, one foot in front of the other, like a waiter in the posh restaurant we went to with Nana near Topplehurst Model Village. And Goffo doesn't move.

He just looks very clever without doing anything.

Which is what Mum said he needed to do.

'How much is the prize?' Natters says.

'Twenty-five pounds,' I say, 'and we're splitting it. Twelve pounds fifty each.'

'I thought of the tray bit,' Natters says. 'I should get some of the money as well.'

Chicken curry cannot cope with this.

'You're all stealing my idea,' Theo shouts.

'But without our help you'll never win,' Natters says. 'You need us, so you have to buy our help.'

'Nat, shush,' Chrissie says under her breath. 'Theo, we'll sort the prize money out after you've won it ...'

But Theo has forgotten what chicken curry tastes like and puts Goffo back on the ground and runs up the garden shouting,

Goffo heads for the apple tree. The excitement is too much for him and he needs a wee.

'Can you two tidy up?' Chrissie says as she follows Theo.

So Natters and I put the plank and the hosepipe away because we are in Years Six and Five and Theo is only in Year Three.

Theo is my brother.

'George,' Theo says, 'what's really wrong with Mum?'

'What do you mean?' I say, and the lamppost we are walking towards suddenly seems a long way away.

'Matthew's mum had a headache last week when I was there and she took a tablet and it went away. Why doesn't Mum's do that?'

I decide not to say anything until we are level with the lamppost.

And while we walk towards it, I think.

Dermo had to make a decision.

Did he tell me about Mum?

Or did he keep it to himself?

And I have to do the same.

It is my choice.

And when we reach the lamppost, I say,

'They think Mum's got cancer.'

And he says,

'How do you know?'

And I say,

'Trust me, I just do.'

I also know Mum is seeing DREW again
tomorrow because I check on the calendar all the
time.

Theo says,

'Is Mum going to die?'

It is the first time we have walked home together
on our own.

No one was around to collect us.

As we do, Theo's hand slips into mine.

And I let him keep it there.

```
FACT NUMBER FORTY-NINE

Dr Winter is one of the best cancer
specialists in the country.
```

Dad buys fish and chips on his way home from the
boring meeting he has been to in Birmingham. Mum is
asleep. So we leave her and sit round the table in
the kitchen to eat them. And as we do Theo
suddenly says,

'Dad, has Mum really got cancer?'

Dad looks straight at him and says,

'Who told you that?'

And Theo says,

'George did.'

And I nearly choke on the chip I am trying to
swallow.

'Who told you?' Dad says to me.

And I say,

'I just thought, because of all her headaches and she's ... ' And I can't think what else to say and there is a tremble in my voice and I want to throttle Theo for opening his big mouth.

Dad lowers his fork so it rests on top of the **crispy batter**.

He closes his eyes.

Like he is walking towards a lamppost and waiting until he is level with it.

Theo and I wait.

Like we are watching his face until our eyes hurt.

Then he says,

'We're going to the hospital tomorrow. Then we'll know.'

'We haven't told you before because we still hope it's not.'

'Is that when you'll see Dr Erin Winter?' I say, and Dad looks at me in surprise.

'How did you know that?' he says.

'Saw her name on the calendar, found her on the internet,' I say, and even as the words come out of my mouth, things are changing all round me.

Because suddenly it is real.

It is not me and Dermo looking at a screen with a name on it and promising, promising, promising not to tell anyone what we found out.

It is actually happening.

Now.

To me.

And Dad.

And Theo.

And Mum.

'Yes,' Dad says quietly. 'We're going to see Dr Erin Winter. And if it is cancer, we'll also know what Mum's treatment will be to get rid of it.'

'Is Mum going to die?' Theo whispers.

'We don't plan for her to die,' Dad says.

I am not hungry any more, but I stab a chip and **slosh it through the puddle of tomato ketchup** on the saucer in front of me and stick it in my mouth and clamp my teeth down on it so the hot potato squashes flat and burns the side of my tongue and my gums and the inside of my mouth.

And I don't care that it hurts.

'I'm not going,' Theo says.

'Theo, it's May. The weather's getting hot. You need some sandals. Or your feet will stink.'

'I hate buying shoes. If I stay here, I won't disturb Mum.'

'Theo, it's shoes then Hawaiian pizza,' Chrissie says and suddenly swings one arm round his legs, hugs him tight with the other and lifts him up.

'Open the front door,' she says to me. 'Now close it,' she says as soon as they are outside.

She kneels down on the drive and holds Theo ever so tight as he sobs into her shoulder.

This is not a tantrum.

This is for real.

Chrissie is crying too.

So I walk down the drive and lean against her green Beetle, being sensible.

I'm good at that.

And as I lean, dark thoughts drift like a raincloud across my brain.

But the rain is made of tiny arrows with pointed tips.

And it is raining inside my head.

When Theo climbs in the car his eyes are red and **blotchy** and he is sniffing. There is a little flower vase next to Chrissie's steering wheel. Usually it has a plastic rose in it. Today it has a sunflower.

'Mum likes those,' Theo whispers.

'I know,' Chrissie says. 'When we get back, do you want to take it to her?'

And Theo lets out a **stuttering** sort of breath and nods.

Chrissie turns the car engine on. She pushes the gear stick into first gear and the car moves forward with the radio playing in the background. I stare out of the window at the houses.

And hate them all.

```
┌─────────────────────────────────────────┐
│                                           │
│      FACT NUMBER FIFTY-ONE                 │
│                                           │
│   A tumour is growing in Mum's brain.      │
│                                           │
└─────────────────────────────────────────┘
```

Sarrington Hospital takes nineteen minutes to drive to
from our house and looks like a huge cube made
of windows and concrete. Mum is there for a few
days and Keith has sent Dad to New York to speak
at a conference. He tried to get out of it, but
couldn't. So Chrissie and Natters are staying at
our house so they can look after me and Theo.

The clock on Chrissie's dashboard reads 18:06 as
we turn into the hospital car park. Different
coloured lines are painted on the floor. We follow
the blue one. It takes us to Hambleton Building
where Mum is on the ground floor, in Ward 1B.

We go through a door with glass in the middle of
it. Inside is a wooden desk with a vase of

sunflowers. I hope they were there yesterday when Mrs Shardini brought Mum in.

In front of us is a wide corridor.

A woman in a dressing gown is walking towards us.

Her slippers drag along the floor.

A man wearing blue trousers and a blue top walks past us.

He has a **stethoscope** round his neck.

He must be a doctor.

The corridor has arrows and notices hanging from the ceiling.

The first sign is Ward 1B.

I am glad we don't have to walk any further.

I don't like this corridor.

It's too big.

Chrissie squirts **anti-bacteria** spray on our hands.

She knows what to do because she spent the afternoon with Mum while we were at school.

A lady in a bed watches us.

There's a tube coming out of her left arm.

It goes to a machine with flashing lights.

'Don't stare,' Chrissie whispers.

A man walks towards us in a pale green top.

'Hi, Chrissie,' he says. His name badge says he is called Pete Heslop.

'Now, which one of you is George?' he says.

'I am,' I whisper, and Pete Heslop says,

'Your mum tells me you know every capital city in the world.'

And I nod, because capitals is my favourite when we play the Visiting Game.

'And you must be Theo,' he says to Theo, who just stares at him and holds Chrissie's hand. He has never been to Ward 1B at Sarrington Hospital before. Neither have I.

We follow Chrissie past beds with people lying on them.

Someone is being sick in a grey bowl.

And I want to go home.

Mum is feeling so ill she can hardly talk.

She holds out her left hand.

'Come round this side,' she whispers.

Her right arm is plugged into a flashing machine and there is blood underneath the sellotape keeping the tube in place.

I want to get on the bed and curl up next to her.

But everyone might think I am silly if I do that.

'Go on, go round,' Chrissie whispers to me.

So I do, and Mum holds my hand and her head is lolling to one side and her eyes are only just open.

'Pete's going to see if he can find a capital city you don't know,' she whispers. Then she says,

'What did you have for supper?' and it is like it hurts when she talks.

'Pasta and meatballs in sauce,' I whisper back.

And she nods and smiles. She knows it's one of my favourites.

'The doctors hope I can **come home** at the weekend,' she says.

I want her home now, telling us stories about Precious Pearson and her aerobic class as we eat roast chicken dinner with crunchy potatoes she has cooked. I want her to be laughing and walking in the woods with Goffo and coming to assemblies at school and working in The Flower Shop and making things with us at the kitchen table before we go to bed.

But now it is like half of her is Mum and the other half is cancer.

And the cancer half tells her to stay in hospital and is making her hair fall out, even though she has had

178

it cut really short. And everyone has to do everything for her.

'Do you want a Malteser?' Mum whispers. 'I asked Mrs Shardini to buy some. They're in my locker.' And she waves her tube arm at a grey locker on the other side of the bed. 'Go round and get them.'

And while I do, Theo stands where I was standing and tells her that the sunflower seeds have started to grow and are sticking out of the compost.

'And George wanted to plant one for Janine,' he says, 'because he fancies her.'

'I do not fancy her,' I say and my cheeks have gone all hot and I want to thump Theo because he has such a big mouth.

And he's in my place next to Mum.

And he's holding her hand.

And all I am holding is the packet of Maltesers Mrs Shardini bought.

'Boys,' Chrissie says, 'your mum does not want to hear you arguing.'

'Tell me what Goffo's been up to,' Mum whispers to Theo.

And after five minutes Mum's eyes are closing and it's time to go.

'Vicky, Jack's coming to see you on his way back from the airport,' Chrissie says and Mum smiles a half-smile as we take it in turns to kiss her very gently and very carefully.

Then we walk away from her bed.

And as we do, dark thoughts hiccough in my brain. And I pretend they are not there.

But they are.

FACT NUMBER FIFTY-THREE

Girls are OK, but I don't fancy them.
At all. Neither does Dermo.

'There's an island called **Tuvalu**,' Pete Heslop says as we pass the nursing station. And for one second I cannot remember what the capital of Tuvalu is.

And then the name pops into my brain because it's a great word to say.

'**Funafuti**.'

'Wow,' Pete says. 'You really are clever. I don't even know where Tuvulu is.'

'South Pacific Ocean. Population eleven thousand,' I say and I am smiling.

'Do you really fancy Janine?' Natters says as we walk back to the car park.

'No,' I say straight away.

'She fancies you,' Natters says.

And I feel a blush **igniting** all over my face.

FACT NUMBER FIFTY-FOUR

Theo has a mouth the size of a dumper truck.

Theo tells his class about us training Goffo for the Summer Showdown and Charmaine Worthington tells The Pukewart about us training Goffo for the Summer Showdown.

'Your freaky dog hasn't a hope in hell of winning,' The Pukewart whispers as we line up for assembly. A blob of his spit lands on the back of my left **earlobe**. 'Just accept it, you're a loser.'

I try and ignore him because he is a bully.

'Oi, you're not deaf,' he carries on. 'You heard what I said. Your dog is a freak.'

My right hand sneaks into a fist and I imagine what it would be like to **smash it** in The Pukewart's face. Blood would shoot out of his nose and go all over his clothes. He would fall backwards and hit his head on the corner of one of the tables so there would be more blood. And he would go to hospital and have drips in both arms and both legs and machines with flashing lights that bleep at him all night to keep him awake.

But I know I will never do it in real life because it is wrong to go round thumping other people and anyway, Mrs Logan is with us now, so The Pukewart shuts up.

'You all right?' she says to me.

I smile at her and nod.

Sometimes it is easier to nod than say what you are really thinking. The Pukewart sits by Mrs Logan's feet in assembly. If he makes any silly noises or prods anyone or writes his name on the wooden floor with spit, he will get a green card and miss playtime. Mrs Logan has the green card in her right hand ready to **shove it in front of his face**.

I love it when she does that.

She did it yesterday because The Pukewart let off when Miss Cortez started talking. Mrs Logan gave him a filthy look, leaned over and whispered,

'Carl Worthington, you are on a warning,' and he giggled at her and that put him straight on a green card.

Miss Cortez **drones on** about how we must behave better because yesterday, some of the Year Six boys lifted up some paving slabs by the wildlife area and could have damaged themselves while they were at it.

After school I wait for Theo by the lamppost. When he arrives, he is smiling to himself, so I **lay into him**.

I say,

'Why did you tell your class about us training Goffo for the Summer Showdown? That was meant to be a secret.'

He looks at me like I am stupid.

'I didn't tell them what we are really doing,' he says. 'I said we were teaching Goffo to jump through a hoop while balancing an egg on his nose. Mr Jennings wrote down what I said on a Post-it note and gave me a house point.'

'But why did you say anything?'

'It was my turn and I couldn't think of anything else.'

'But it's a lie.'

'So?'

'But Show and Tell is when you share something that is important to you.'

'So?'

Then I say,

'Do you always tell a load of porkies in Show and Tell?'

'Yeah. Don't you?'

The thought has never even crossed my mind.

Nana lets Granddad go on eBay. He buys a new car for my electric racing track which is on my bedroom floor. Granddad also buys Theo a remote controlled tarantula spider. It climbs up furniture and rolls on its back then **waggles** its legs in the air. Ivan and Goffo think the tarantula is a new friend with **spindly** legs like theirs. They lick its bottom until Nana says,

'Ivan, off!'

And Ivan walks backwards and lies at her feet.

'Good dog,' she says and strokes his ears with her left hand. Then she barks,

'Goffo, off!'

Goffo looks at her like she is a **boiled slug** and starts racing round the living room and jumping on the sofa.

So Nana tries to wither him.

But he ignores her and carries on dancing and it is hilarious because Nana's face is like **thunder**.

'Boys, stop laughing,' she says. 'Goffo, off the sofa. Get down!'

'It'll take him fffffourteen minutes to get off the sofa,' Theo giggles.

'No it won't,' Nana says. 'Goffo . . . Down . . . Now.'

And Goffo still ignores her.

Until she grabs him with both hands and lifts him up so his eyes are level with hers. His legs paddle in the air like he is swimming. Then he realises how high up he is and freezes.

'Nana,' Theo says, 'he doesn't like being held up that high.'

And Nana says,

'Then he will learn very quickly how to behave himself.'

And Theo and I just watch.

It is like **Cruella de Vil** has moved in as Goffo stays absolutely still.

Then, very slowly, Nana lowers him to the floor.

'Goffo,' she says, when his paws are nearly back on the floor, 'you are going to sort yourself out. That is not a choice. It is what is going to happen.' And Goffo's little head drops and he studies the bits of fluff on the carpet as she finally lowers him right down.

'Good dog!' Nana says and strokes his head and I am waiting for her to get out a doggie star chart.

Only she doesn't.

Instead, she looks at me and Theo.

'While I am here,' she says, 'Goffo will behave in the same way Mrs Rentop trained Ivan. So there will be no ... more ... pig's ears. He can have one Doggie Treat every now and then and a proper bone to keep his teeth in good working order.'

Goffo turns his head and looks at me.

Then he looks at Theo.

No one moves.

Nana stares at Goffo.

We stare at Nana.

'Now go and sit by your brother,' she says.

And Goffo walks over to where Ivan is waiting.

On his way he sighs.

Then he lowers his little bottom on to the carpet.

He has been completely withered.

Beaten.

Reduced to nothing.

And Nana only arrived half an hour ago.

FACT NUMBER FIFTY-SIX

Nana is in charge. Of everything.

'Theo, where's your book bag?' she says, and Theo knows he will have to sit next to her with a cushion on his lap and read his book. At least he will have a new signature in his home-school book. Chrissie Cooper, Jack Warren, Vicky Warren, George Warren, Natters Cooper, Sharon Harris, Elise Clutterbuck, and now ... Joyce Cooper.

'I want Granddad to sign it next,' Theo says. 'He will write Arthur Cooper. And then Mrs Shardini, who wears a bikini and ... '

'Theo, we'll have none of that,' Nana says, cutting him off.

And Theo starts giggling.

'You can stop the giggling as well,' she says. 'Now what page number are you up to?'

'Fffffourteen,' he says without looking.

'You're not,' Nana says. 'You said the number fourteen because, for some reason, you and George find it funny. So please stop saying it.'

And Theo says,

'Yes, Nana.'

Because there is nothing else to say.

FACT NUMBER FIFTY-SEVEN

Helping charts are really the same as star charts.

Nana lets us have crisps in our packed lunch box as a treat when we have five stickers on our helping charts. She says star charts are for school and helping charts are different because they have big stickers with aliens and hedgehogs on them. Which are not stars.

Theo gets a sticker if his bedroom is tidy, his outside shoes are on the sheet of polythene by the back door and he doesn't **pass wind, belch, burp or pick his nose** when Nana is in the room. I get a sticker if I clean my teeth without dribbling toothpaste spit out of my mouth, lay the table before supper and help brush the dogs.

And when she is with us, we know that she will be outside school at the end of the day. And when we get home, Mum is usually awake and downstairs and wants to know what we have been doing. Her cancer drugs make her sleepy, but she beat me at Scrabble yesterday and I tried really hard to win.

When I was putting the letters away she said,

'A man went to a farm and saw . . . a tractor.' And we haven't played the Visiting Game for ages. And I smiled inside and said,

'Lots of mud.'

And she said,

'And he saw . . . a chicken.'

'**Derbyshire Redcap**,' I said, remembering when we went to Thendon Wildlife Park last summer.

'And . . . a red panda.'

She smiled at me. The red pandas were my favourite and she and I spent ages watching them **clamber** all over their tree.

As Mum smiled, saliva dribbled out of the side of her mouth and she wiped it away with a tissue.

Granddad teaches me to play **chess** and reads his newspaper at the kitchen table and **slurps** his coffee and goes **boss-eyed** to make us laugh if Nana isn't looking.

We are allowed on the PlayStation for an hour each day and can watch television for the same amount of time, unless it is a something Granddad wants to watch, or a football match. Then we are allowed to watch for longer. Granddad likes quiz shows and cookery programmes and we sit together, all curled up on the sofa. Henry Snail and Gregory Grasshopper usually watch with us, and Nana brings in popcorn and sticks of carrot as long as we don't drop bits on the sofa and still eat our suppers.

And we help Nana make cakes and brownies, and decorate them with sugar icing and chocolate buttons.

And she brings cardboard boxes back from the supermarket so we can turn them into garages for our cars.

And we go to the park and she buys us a Frisbee each which the dogs love chasing after.

And Nana makes our **favourite meals** and finds the pairs to our socks and reads stories to us before we go to bed.

And she hoovers the carpets and my bedroom is tidy and our clothes are washed and we play games, as long as Theo isn't silly with the dice.

Somehow it is safer with Nana being in charge.

And the dark thoughts are still there, but not as much.

> ## FACT NUMBER FIFTY-NINE
>
> *The word* terminal *means you don't get better.*

Mum fell over and is back in hospital for a few days. Dad comes home after seeing her, kicks the zimmer frame which lives in the hall when Mum isn't here, throws his car keys in the bowl on the little window sill, walks straight to the kitchen and shuts the door.

The biscuits we have just made are cooking in the oven on the middle shelf. Nana is making sure they behave themselves while she gets supper ready. We are having **broccoli bake with cheese breadcrumbs**. Theo and I grated the cheese. It's **Red Leicester** and is bright orange. We are now in the back room playing with the new castle Granddad made with us. It has flags and a

drawbridge and four towers. He bought some
knights, a dragon and a princess from the toy
shop. Theo cut the princess's hair off, drew a pair
of glasses on her in felt-tipped pen and called her
Princess Willy. Nana says that name is short for
Princess Wilhelmina.

I am drawing bricks on the cardboard castle walls
in black pen. It is taking me ages but looks really
good. Nana showed me how to draw them so
they look like real bricks that **overlap** each other.
Theo wasn't very good at drawing bricks, so he is
now doing a jigsaw with Granddad because
Granddad loves doing jigsaws, as long as he can
have a sultana every time he puts a piece in the
right place. I have a sultana every time I draw ten
bricks.

'Stay here,' Granddad says quietly. 'Give your dad
a bit of space, then we'll find out what's
happened.'

A few minutes later he stands up and goes to the
kitchen.

Theo and I wait.

Neither of us says anything.

Granddad comes back in.

'Do you want to come to the kitchen?' he says.

We sit round the table.

Dad has been crying.

So has Nana.

Mum is terminal.

Which means Dr Erin Winter cannot get rid of the tumour.

Mum is staying in hospital for a day or two.

Then she is coming home.

She is going to die.

They don't know when.

It depends on how fast the tumour decides to grow.

Theo climbs on to Dad's lap.

My legs are too long to do that.

So Dad puts his right arm round me.

And pulls me in, so I am very close.

I can feel his heart beating against my ear.

Nana and Granddad are sitting opposite.

And we all cry.

Because we all love her.

Dark thoughts have sharp fingernails.

They are shoving them round my brain.

Henry Snail is feeling scared.

And lonely.

And frightened.

And I have got to be extra-sensible.

And then I wonder, again, if Mum is ill because of me.

FACT NUMBER SIXTY-ONE

£25.00 divided by three is two lots of £8.33 (which Natters and I will have) and one lot of £8.34 (which Theo will have, because he was the one who thought of entering the competition in the first place).

Nana says,

'Why doesn't Ivan become part of the pet competition trick as well?'

And Theo says,

'No,' straight away because he thinks Nana is after the prize money.

'You can borrow Ivan for free,' she says.

So Theo says, 'Yes.'

And I say, 'Yes.'

And Natters says, 'Yes.'

So Nana now joins in helping with the trick, which is brilliant because she knows about all sorts of things.

The Summer Showdown Pet Competition is written in big red letters on the calendar in the kitchen.

And we plan to win.

And everyone is going to help.

And Mum says she is going to do everything she possibly can to be there as well.

I help Dad and Granddad make a proper see-saw out of wood and we paint it bright yellow because that is Mum's favourite colour. And Nana writes out a list of instructions to help us learn what to do. She has to do this because she has changed the beginning of the trick.

1. Make sure Ivan is in the yellow cardboard box.

2. George clips the cardboard box (with Ivan inside it) on the bottom end of the see-saw plank.

3. Natters pushes the high end of the plank down to the ground and Goffo walks on to it. Ivan is now at the top, inside the yellow box.

4. Goffo walks down the plank then jumps into the cardboard box with Ivan.

5. Natters takes Goffo out of the box and puts him on Theo's tray (which has a treat on it).

6. Natters takes Ivan out of the box and puts him on George's tray (which also has a treat on it). As no one knows Ivan is in the box, everyone will laugh as it will look like Goffo has doubled himself. Pause while they clap.

7. Theo and George walk round the see-saw in opposite directions with the dogs on their trays.

8. When they meet, they bow to each other like sumo wrestlers and lower the trays to the ground.

9. Goffo and Ivan run to Natters who has moved to the side.

10. Theo and George stand apart and

turn their trays over. George's tray reads COME HERE in Arsenal red and Theo's tray reads GO TO THE RED TRAY in *Chelsea* blue.

11. Goffo barks at Theo's tray then runs to the red tray. Ivan follows him.

12. Natters unclips the cardboard box and puts it on the floor below the raised end of the see-saw. Theo takes the dogs to the lower end of the see-saw. George holds the lower end down.

13. Both dogs run up the plank and jump into the yellow cardboard box.

'That will be really good,' Nana says when we finish practising. Theo and I high-five each other. The Worthingtons might as well stay at home. 'And now,' she says, 'let's plant out the sunflowers along the fence. I have bought some canes to put in the soil to make them grow straight.'

So Theo and I help her do that and when we have finished, I cut a strip off a blue plastic bag and wrap it round the stem of my sunflower.

'That's to stop Goffo weeing on it,' I say. 'He'll just bark at it instead.'

'Do you really think that will stop him?' Nana says.

One week later, my sunflower has grown two new leaves and all the others have only grown one.

FACT NUMBER SIXTY-TWO

Granddad often buys the local newspaper as well as The Times.

Granddad stops reading the newspaper and looks up.

'What's the name of that boy who's a bully in your class?' he says.

'Carl Worthington,' I say, as I scrape honey off my plate with my **index finger**.

'Has he got a brother?' Granddad asks.

'Yes.'

'What's he called?'

'Harry.'

'Hmmmm,' Granddad says and turns the page.

'What's he done?' I say.

'Nothing,' Granddad says.

So I know he has done something.

*Sharon tells Dermo what Harry
Worthington has done.*

At school, Dermo says is,

'Have you heard about Harry Worthington?'

And I say,

'Granddad wouldn't tell me.'

And Dermo says,

'He's been arrested for dog baiting.'

'What's that?' Skye says.

'Two dogs fight each other and people bet which
is going to win.'

'Harry Worthington does that?' I say.

And all I can think about is if Goffo and Ivan started fighting each other in our back room. Nana would go,

'Stop!' and they would both freeze. Then she would say,

'Sit!' and they would both sit and that would be the end of it.

Mrs Logan says she does not want to hear anyone talking about it.

At all.

'Carl is not in school today,' she says. 'When he comes back, no one mentions it or asks him about it. Harry Worthington has been arrested. It does not mean he is guilty.'

We all stare at her. It must be horrible having a brother who could do something like getting dogs to try and kill each other.

Because Dermo says that's what dogs that fight, if they are being baited, do.

Elise and Grandpa give Mum some money to buy
a water feature so she can look at it through the
patio window. We go to Haven Garden Centre
which has a play area for children next to a café.
Dad's shed came from here, our trampoline came
from here and so did Mum's bird table.

Dad helps Mum out of our car and into her
wheelchair. Theo wants to go to the children's
section behind the spades and wheelbarrows. He's
hoping Grandpa will buy him a water soaker.

'They sell wellies here, don't they?' Elise says
to me. 'I need a new pair.'

'But Mum and Dad will be on their own,' I say.

'I know,' Elise says. 'We can meet them in the café later.'

The wellie boots are either black or green.

'They're a bit boring,' Elise whispers. 'Let's go and find the sculptures. Your dad said they're by the sheds.'

There are some **spheres** and stars made out of brass, and curved bits of metal with patterns painted on them, and angels with wings balancing on one leg. Next to them is one gnome holding a fishing rod, four clay snails and three painted wooden butterflies in a basket.

'They're boring as well,' Elise says and sits down on a garden bench priced two hundred and ninety-five pounds, 'And it's very uncomfortable.'

I sit next to her. Metal bars dig into my bottom.

'I like places that are boring,' she says.

I look at her and frown.

'If it's boring,' she says, 'you can think of ways to make it better. Like if this bench was made of jelly, it'd be more comfortable because our bottoms would mould into it.'

'Or the gnome could be two metres tall so children could hide inside it,' I say.

'Or those flowers could burp if anyone walked past them,' she says.

So we play this new game.

It is like the Visiting Game, only different, and you have to say how you would make something better. So we make flowers stink of **putrefied** seaweed, sheds built of elastic and hanging baskets bounce on springs like they are **pogo-sticks for birds**.

The sun is shining and we are laughing out loud because Elise is funny. And when we stop playing Make It Better, I say,

'How old were you when your mum died?'

'Ten,' she says.

'What did she die of?'

'Lorry drove into her car. My little brother was with her.'

'How old was he?'

'Alan was six.'

'Were you there as well?'

'No, I was visiting my dad. He took me to the hospital but it was too late.'

We sit for a few minutes, not saying anything. Then she says,

'How are you feeling about your mum?'

And I take a deep breath because dark thoughts are waking up and we are not laughing any more.

The loneliness and the scared ache in my tummy have woken up too.

A robin lands on one of the angel's shoulders. It waggles its tail. It looks silly and I wish it would fly away.

'I don't know,' I say.

And I don't know because there is so much going on, I never have time to think.

When he's home, Dad looks after Mum.

So does Nana.

Nana looks after me and Theo as well.

So does Dad, when he's not looking after Mum.

Granddad looks after us too when he's not fitting kitchens in people's houses.

So does Chrissie when she's not at work.

And Grandpa and Elise visit whenever they can.

And everyone keeps doing things with us.

Which is OK.

Because while we are doing things, the dark thoughts look after themselves and stay asleep.

Only Elise has just woken them up and it is the middle of the day.

Elise's cardigan is soft and fluffy.

'What are you really thinking?' she says.

'Nothing,' I say.

She looks at me.

'You must be thinking something,' she says.

And suddenly I do know what I'm thinking.

Because the dark thoughts are buzzing and jerking and hanging on to my brain, like they're tearing it apart.

The robin sticks its wings out and flies off.

And as it does, I say it.

216

Out loud.

I say the darkest thought.

The one that keeps coming back.

The one I hate the most.

The one that really, really scares me.

And the words stick in the back of my throat.

Because they don't really want to come out.

'I ... keep thinking ... Mum's ill ... because of me,' I whisper.

I have said it.

And as I do, the darkest thought empties its stomach.

Like acid trickling over the inside of my skull.

It's cold.

And a tear wants to roll.

I tell the tear to stay where it is.

Only it doesn't.

And some of its friends want to follow it.

I tell them to stay where they are too.

But they all ignore me.

Elise's cardigan is pale yellow.

I feel it against my cheeks as she puts her arm round me.

'George,' she says, 'it is not your fault your mum is ill. It never has been. It never will be. She's ill because she's ill. And that's it.'

And this isn't the Make It Better game any more.

You can't make tears into something better.

They're just tears.

They fall.

They make your cheeks wet.

I can't do this being sensible any more.

I pretend when I'm at school.

When everything is busy, busy, busy.

And Dermo is my friend and he looks after me.

But he doesn't really understand.

No one does.

Because no one else's mum has a brain tumour.

No one else's mum.

Is dying.

And mine is.

And when I go to bed.

I don't sleep.

Because all the time, Mum is getting worse.

Like she can't smile any more.

Because her lips won't move to the right position.

And her hands are thin.

And she moves them slowly.

And Dad has to help her climb the stairs.

And the darkest thought makes me think that somehow it is my fault.

'It is not your fault,' Elise whispers. 'George, it's not.'

And she kisses the top of my head.

Like Mum used to do.

'I'm scared,' I whisper.

'I felt scared too,' Elise whispers back.

The metal bars from the seat really dig into my bottom. Elise **ferrets** in her bag to find a tissue.

'What's your favourite flower?' she says, handing it to me.

'Sunflower,' I say and the words come out in a big gulp, 'because they're big ... and bright and yellow.'

And because they are Mum's favourite.

Suddenly I want to hold Elise's hand because next year sunflowers will grow all over the world and wave in the breeze and turn their heads towards the sun.

And Mum won't see them.

Because Mum will be somewhere else.

And the feeling like I am all alone won't go away.

But Elise knows what it feels like, because her mum died too.

The gnome with the fishing rod has a grin on his face like he is passing wind but doesn't want anyone to know about it. Elise says,

'That gnome is very expensive too.' Then she says, 'Shall we go and find the café?'

And I nod.

'What's your favourite word?' I ask her.*

Right now, I like the word **café** because it usually means **chocolate cake** as well.

'Hmmm,' she says. 'It would have to be a word that sounded like itself. They used to be called onomatopoeias.'

'They still are,' I say.

---

*At school my favourite word is **dilapidated**. I got bored with hilarious.

'Splat,' she says. And I say,

'**Mo-not-o-nous**,' in a monotonous sort of way.

'Moo,' she says.

'Whoops!' I say back.

'Ka-pow!'

'S-l-o-w,' I say very slowly.

'What about this one,' she says. '**Fffff ... art**!'

She did not say breaking wind or passing wind or letting off or blowing off or letting one rip or wifta. Elise Clutterbuck said the word **fart**.

And I say,

'**Fart** is one of my favourite words as well.'

'You know you and Theo giggle when one of you says fourteen, do you say that instead of the word **fart**?'

I nod.

'It's because everyone **farts** fourteen times a day,' I say.

'I thought it was something like that,' Elise says.

'Did you know **farts come out of your bottom at seven miles an hour?**'

And I didn't know that.

But I do now.

FACT NUMBER SIXTY-SEVEN

Today is Sunday.

Dad opens the front door and lets Fran in. She works for the hospice where Mum will go when she is too ill for us to look after her at home. Fran sometimes helps Mum get dressed and makes sure she is drinking her super-protein drinks that live on the top shelf of the fridge. Theo and I tried one of Mum's drinks the other day. Nana was in the garden inspecting the sunflowers and getting the washing in and Theo was helping himself to a drink of milk. He took out Mum's carton. It had a straw sticking out of it to stop Mum slopping it on her clothes. We both had a **slurp**. It was revolting. I just about managed to swallow mine, but Theo spat his out and Goffo licked it off the kitchen floor.

So now he is a super-proteined dog and might grow a pair of underpants and become superdog and fly through the air.

'Enjoy sports day tomorrow,' Fran says as she leaves. 'Your mum is really looking forward to watching you both.'

'I'm in the wellie throwing race,' Theo says. 'I'm dead good.' And he spins round and round then pretends to hurl a wellie. And in his little brain he is the world champion wellie thrower and receives medals and has a girlfriend who lets him eat **Marmite sandwiches with bogeys** in whenever he likes.

'The wellie went up in the sky,' Theo says in his limerick voice, and pauses.

So I say,

'It went up very high.'

Then he says,

'It hit a cloud and was very loud.'

And now I have to do the last line and say,

'And they all ate chicken pie.'

'That's rubbish,' Theo says.

'I know,' I say.

That's because we haven't made up a rhyme for ages.

Mum does not like it too hot.

And it isn't.

She doesn't like it too cold either.

And it isn't.

We sit in lines along one side of the running track. Mum and Dad are on the other side, facing us. Dad has moved one of the chairs to fit Mum's wheelchair in. He is holding the camera and Sharon is next to them.

Mum looks across and slowly waves her hand.

I wave back at her.

My wave is faster than hers.

'That your mum in a wheelchair?' The Pukewart says and I nod.

'What's she in that for?'

'She's ill,' I say.

'What's she got?'

'Brain tumour,' I say.

'Where did she get that from?' he says.

And I wish he would shut up.

My fingers wrap round the grass in front of me. I pull three blades out of the ground and lay them across my left knee.

'You're making that up,' he says, and his mum is sitting next to AJ's mum in a floppy sun hat, like she is on the beach. And she is chewing gum because her jaws are going up and down and if Nana saw her she would wither her and say her face looks like a washing machine with underwear in.

229

I wish Nana was here now.

She would wither The Pukewart as well and I would
love her forever because his mum will be at sports
day next year, wearing a big floppy hat and
chewing gum.

And my mum won't.

My left hand, the one that just pulled up three
blades of grass, clenches into a fist and I imagine
shoving it in The Pukewart's face.

And as I think that, Mrs Logan lowers her chair
behind us.

'I see your mum's over there, George,' she says.
'That is really good, isn't it?' And I nod.

I am good at nodding.

It's easier than talking.

'What's Theo doing this afternoon?' she asks.

'Wellie throwing.'

'That's the first event,' she says. 'He'll be on in a
minute.'

Mrs Logan lays a green card on her lap and gives The Pukewart **a filthy look** as Mr Jennings, who is in charge of sports day, calls the wellie throwers to walk to the starting line.

The wellie throwers line up for their one throw. Gurpal Singh has a big black wellie and he is first. His wellie lands between the lines of children on one side of the track and the rows of parents sitting on the other. Everyone on our side of the track cheers because that is what children do.

The parents and grandparents on the other side clap.

Theo is next.

He has a bright green wellie with frog's eyes at the front.

He stands **like a gladiator** and does a little dance.

I look up at Mrs Logan.

She is smiling.

I look at Dad.

He is holding the camera.

I look at Mum.

She is staring at Theo.

Her mouth is slightly open.

She should be leaning forward and talking to Sharon and laughing and moving her arms and getting ready to clap.

Only she isn't.

The brain tumour has decided that today she can just stare.

Theo rocks his body backwards and forwards.

Then he spins round three times.

He lets go of the wellie.

It goes straight up, **like a lift in a shop**.

Theo carries on spinning.

The wellie hovers in the air, like it is making up its mind what to do next.

Then it drops.

Straight down.

Theo has spun round five times.

He is dizzy.

The wellie lands.

On Theo's head.

And everyone claps and cheers and laughs.

And Theo bursts into tears.

His big moment to win the wellie throwing.

And he has blown it.

Though Theo is the centre of attention and everyone is talking about him.

So it's not all bad.

We watch it later on at home.

All five of us on the sofa.

Vicky Warren, Theo Warren, Jack Warren, George Warren and Goffo.

FACT NUMBER SEVENTY

June 28ᵗʰ is Mum's fortieth birthday.

We celebrate Mum's birthday by going to
Thendon Wildlife Park. Theo, Natters and I
have a day off school. Dad has a day off work
too.

Thendon is like Topplehurst Model Village
because Goffo and Ivan are allowed in as long as
they are kept on a lead and do not scare the
animals.

Red pandas normally live in the Himalayas and
China, capital city **Beijing**. They're little and
orangey-brown with stripy tails.

Goffo takes one look at them and sneezes.

'Goffo, be quiet,' Nana says. Goffo looks at her and is quiet and then trots along beside Mum with his pink lead hanging from the handles of her wheelchair.

It is when we are by the purple-faced langurs that the excitement really begins. Langurs come from Sri Lanka and eat leaves, flowers and seeds. They are also called bear monkeys and are an endangered **species**. Nana reads information about them to Theo, who is not listening because he is watching the langurs scratch their bottoms.

A man in a Thendon Wildlife Park T-shirt comes up to Dad and asks if he can have a word. Dad checks what Theo is doing. He is standing next to Nana so must be behaving himself.

A few minutes later Dad whispers something to Mum who wobbles her head. She does not do proper nods any more.

She does not wave, either.

'Fancy going on television?' Dad asks me and Theo and Natters. 'They're making a programme

about langurs and the wildlife park's breeding
programme.'

They want to release langurs back into the wild
and need a family to say what they think about it.

Theo does a big fat wifta in excitement and Natters opens her shoulder bag and takes out a brush to make sure her hair is OK. Nana checks our shirts are tucked in.

The Thendon Wildlife Park man fetches a lady called Sophia who is carrying a camera. A man called Bob Shuttles has a huge pole with a grey fluffy microphone on the end of it. He says 'Hello' and explains what he wants us to do.

We practise walking towards the cage where the langurs live, talking to each other. Granddad tells me he is going to buy everyone an **ice cream** when we get back to the shop. And I say,

'I want a strawberry one,' and he says,

'I'm going to buy everyone an ice cream when we get back to the shop.' And I say,

'I want a strawberry one.' And he says,

'I'm going to buy everyone . . . ' and I start laughing.

Sophia tells Theo to stop kicking the gravel as it makes a nasty noise on the soundtrack. So we do it again and this time Sophia is happy and asks for the children to **step forward** and be interviewed.

We stand in front of the cage with langurs hanging behind us. Sophia tells us to ignore what they are doing and concentrate on saying how we have always loved langurs and how great Thendon Wildlife Park is for breeding them and putting some back in the wild.

Theo has to repeat one of his sentences because he scratches his left nostril as he is speaking. Then we are finished. Sophia says she will let Dad know when the programme will be broadcast if

Dad sends an e-mail to the address on the little card she gives him.

It will be in September sometime.

'That's something to look forward to,' Nana says and Mum says,

'You are going on television, and I saw it.'

In front of her, Theo hums to himself and in his little mind he is in Hollywood with a **host of bodyguards** and a limo and a house with a swimming pool.

Because he is going to be a famous person.

FACT NUMBER SEVENTY-TWO

The Visiting Game is something just Mum and I play.

We go to the **Insect and Invertebrate House** next. It is smelly and **humid** and like being in a tunnel. The dogs aren't happy. Neither is Mum. So we hitch both leads to the wheelchair handles and I wheel her, and them, back outside.

I park the wheelchair by a little wall and hold the carton and straw while she has a drink.

'Thanks,' she whispers and lets her head fall back on the pillow at the back of her chair. Ever so slowly she reaches out and wraps her thin spindly fingers round mine.

I don't ever want to leave Thendon Wildlife Park.

Because when we get home, Dad will carry Mum upstairs and she'll stay there all of tomorrow because today will have worn her out.

'A family visit Thendon and see ... a chameleon,' she whispers.

'Lizard,' I say back.

'And ... a scorpion,' she whispers.

'**Arachnid**. Four pairs of legs, stinger at the end of its tail.'

'**I love you**,' she whispers.

'**And I love you**,' I whisper back.

And I do.

And we sit in the sunshine.

And just for one minute I am not sharing her with anyone else.

It is the last time we ever play the Visiting Game. I write about it in the book we make with Fran. It is a book about all the special things we have done with Mum so we will be able to remember her.

I write about the snail as well, because as Mum and I sit there, Theo suddenly shoots out of the Insect and Invertebrate House waving a piece of paper.

'Rambo, Rambo, I've got Rambo!' he yells.

'Who is Rambo?' I ask.

'My tarantula! Nana just bought him for me.'

'Theo, where is he going to live?'

'By my bed.'

'Your bed?' And I imagine Theo waking up in the middle of the night with a tarantula sticking its legs up his nose scraping bogeys out for its breakfast.

'Show me the piece of paper,' I say.

He gives me a picture of a spider with orange and black stripes sitting on top of a grey stone. And for five pounds Theo has provided him with food and care for ten whole days. The spider stays in

Thendon Wildlife Park and Theo will never see it again.

Dad and Natters are walking towards us now. Natters has bought food for a chameleon called Terry.

'Do you want one?' Dad asks me.

So now on my chest of drawers next to my triceratops and the Arsenal lamp is a picture of Ethel the Giant African Land Snail. Henry doesn't mind there being another snail around because Henry lives on my pillow.

There's also an emperor penguin with its neck curling down to look at its baby. It's a cuddly toy and I don't actually need it because I've got Henry, but Granddad bought it for me at the gift shop to remind me of a really special day.

WATSON PARK PRIMARY SCHOOL
SUMMER SHOWDOWN

Saturday July 9th
Pet Talent Competition
First Round: 1.30 – 2.30 in the Square Tent
Final Five: 3 – 3.30 in the Main Arena
Karaoke Singing Competition
Cake stall
Side shows including the Electric Bump Ride
Sydney Morris Blues Band
Beer and Burger Tent
£1 admission
Free programme

On the kitchen table are:

- two trays
- my yellow waistcoat
- Theo's yellow waistcoat
- the yellow cardboard box

The see-saw base and plank with a hook at one end to hold the cardboard box in place are by the back door.

Ivan lies quietly on a newspaper spread over the kitchen table while Nana brushes his coat. He wags his tail when she has finished. Nana clips a little sunflower she made on the top of his head and kisses his nose. He looks very cute.

'Now, where is Goffo?' she says.

Goffo has disappeared.

Completely.

Dad looks upstairs.

Granddad looks downstairs.

I look in the cupboard under the stairs.

'I know who can help us find Goffo,' Theo says.

'Who?' Nana asks.

'His brother,' Theo says and lifts Ivan off the table. Then he sticks his ear next to Ivan's mouth as if Ivan is talking to him.

'He says his brother is at the bottom of the garden but will only come back in the house if Ivan fetches him.'

Nana frowns.

Theo is up to something.

'Why can't you just fetch him?' Nana says.

'Because he won't come unless Ivan tells him,' Theo says.

'Mmmm,' Nana says. 'If you take Ivan in the garden, you must keep him in your arms. I don't want him getting untidy or muddy.'

'He won't,' Theo says and walks out of the back door with Ivan looking over his shoulder.

My brother returns a couple of minutes later carrying a scruffy dog without a sunflower.

'Where's Ivan?' Nana asks. 'He's not getting dirty, is he?'

'I told him to stay and I'm going back to fetch him now,' he says, and smiles **innocently**.

'Theo, what are you up to?' Nana says.

'Nothing,' Theo says.

Which means something.

I watch him **slowly saunter** down the garden. He is being too helpful and too smiley, but I haven't got a clue why.

And anyway, Chrissie and Natters have arrived with Janine, who is wearing a sparkly top and a pair of leggings.

*I do not fancy Janine, even if she
fancies me.*

Natters is already wearing her leotard. In her bag
is a clown bowler hat with a plastic sunflower
sticking out of the top. She and Janine sit at one
end of the kitchen table. Janine opens her bag
and takes out eyeshadow and lipstick and
blusher.

'Do you want some make-up on?' she asks Theo
when he returns with Ivan in his arms.

'Get lost,' Theo says.

'Oi, don't get shirty with me,' Janine says back.
She's dead **feisty**. I like that word. Mrs Logan gave
it to us last week and we had to put it in a
sentence. I wrote 'The feisty princess hit the

249

dragon on the nose.' Then I looked up the word 'hit' in the thesaurus and wrote **clouted** instead. Mrs Logan gave me a house point.

Janine is wearing pink nail varnish and her hair is in a ponytail. She asks me if I'd like some blue eyeshadow and I say, 'No way,' and she and Natters giggle.

'Go on, let her put some on you,' Natters says and Janine blushes bright red and Natters pretends her hand is a fan and waves it in front of Janine's cheeks. So I go into the back room to read my football magazine in peace.

I can't be doing with all that giggling.

Elise and Grandpa arrive just before lunch. Elise comes straight in the back room with two little boxes.

'My latest design,' she says. 'There's one for each of you.'

Inside the boxes are sharpeners. Theo's still looks like a dinosaur. Mine still looks like Goffo. The blade is still inside the animals' bottoms, but both animals now stand on boxes with a little drawer to catch the sharpenings that drop out of their tummies.

'Try them out,' Elise says.

I find a pencil and twist it in the sharpener.

Nothing happens.

'Keep going,' Elise says.

I twist it again.

Nothing happens.

I twist it until the lead is sharp and the tip touches a sound sensor.

As it does the pencil sharpener lets off a rumble of a wifta.

Theo and I shriek with laughter.

Theo's dinosaur does the same thing.

'**Inspired by Goffo**,' she says.

Elise is so clever.

*Doing something together is more fun
than doing something on your own.*

Half an hour later we are ready to go.

Chrissie is first, pushing Mum's wheelchair along
the pavement.

Behind them are Natters and Janine, making sure
their bags stay on their shoulders.

Next is Dad with the see-saw plank under his left
arm. Theo is holding Dad's right hand which
makes Theo's left shirt sleeve drop a little. He is
wearing the all-singing, all-dancing waterproof
watch Elise and Grandpa gave him for his
birthday. He has never worn that watch before.

And what I want to know is ... why is he wearing
it today?

I cannot work out what he is up to.

Neither can Nana who keeps looking like she is keeping an eye on him.

Then there's Elise, carrying one handle of her bag. She cannot close it because it has the trays in. Grandpa is holding the other handle and walking beside her.

Granddad is behind them, wheeling the see-saw base on Theo's skateboard.

I am next to him holding a pink lead in my right hand. Goffo is being really sensible because Nana is just behind him.

And she is in charge of the yellow box with Ivan sitting inside it.

At school, people keep stopping to say, 'Hello,' and 'How are you,' and things like that to Mum. So we leave her and Chrissie and go to the Square Tent to register **See Double Saw**, which is what Natters and I decide to call our act because Theo can't think of a clever name like that is.

Kai's dad writes our names and ages on his chart and asks us to return at two-oh-five to show our act to the judges. I notice Charmaine and Carl Worthington are first on the list. Their act is called Whiskey, which is the name of their cat, and their ages are eight and ten.

Esme Abbot's gecko is third. She is aged nine and her act is called Galloping Gecko. Reuben Potter from Year Three has a rat. He is eighth.

We are ninth.

Natalie Cooper, Theo Warren, George Warren.

See Double Saw.

Aged eight, ten and eleven.

They are running late and we have to wait outside the tent for a little while before Kai's dad tells us to go in. Natters has Goffo on his lead. He sees the judges, lifts one of his front legs up and tries to scratch his nose. Rusty and Carmel smile at him, then at us. The other judge is a reporter from the *Weekly Herald* newspaper and his eyebrows twitch when he smiles.

I pull the see-saw base off the skateboard and look round for Theo, who has the plank. He is grinning at the judges, which is what Nana told him to do.

Natters helps me slot the centre of the plank across the balancing bar on the base. Then we put the yellow cardboard box with Ivan sitting quietly inside it on the lower part of the plank before she hands Theo and me the trays.

We are ready.

'So whose idea is this trick?' Rusty asks. 'It looks very interesting.'

'Mine,' Theo says straight away.

'Well,' Natters says, 'it was Theo's idea to enter the competition, George thought of using a see-saw. Then I added the tray bit.'

'And the dog's name is?' Carmel asks.

'Goffo,' Natters says.

'How did you choose that name?' Rusty asks.

'Mum chose it because she loves sunflowers and wanted to name him after Vincent van Gogh,' I say.

'And Ivan is his brother and he joined in because Nana came to live with us because Mum is ill,' Theo pipes up and Natters and I both turn our heads and stare at him because he is giving away the trick before we have even started.

'And where is Ivan?' the reporter asks and Natters says, **cool as a cucumber,**

'You'll have to wait and see,' and smiles at the judges, who smile back at her.

'Did you say your mother is ill?' the reporter asks.

'She's got cancer,' Theo says. 'A brain tumour. Lots of people get better from cancer, but she has a sort where you don't get better.'

'Is she here today?' he asks and we all nod.

'Yes, but she's not Natters' mum,' Theo says, 'she's my mum and she's George's mum. Natters comes to our house when Chrissie looks after us because Chrissie is Mum's sister.'

Theo is like **motor-mouth** today.

'And where did you get Goffo from?' Carmel asks.

'The Dog Rescue Centre near where our grandparents live,' I say and Carmel nods and the reporter's pen wiggles.

'And are you all eleven and under?' Rusty says, looking at Natters.

'My birthday is in September and I am eleven and in Year Six,' she smiles back.

'Though you do look older,' Rusty says.

'My mum's outside if you want to check,' Natters says politely.

'That's all right,' Rusty smiles, 'we'll believe you.'

And then she asks us to perform our trick.

> ## FACT NUMBER SEVENTY-EIGHT
>
> *The Final Five acts from the first round are posted on the tent at a quarter to three, in no particular order.*

We are the fifth act listed. The Worthingtons are also through to the Final Five and will go just before us.

'So what time will that be?' Theo says.

'About three twenty-five,' Granddad says. And straight away, Theo lifts his wrist to check the time.

And smiles as he lowers his arm.

'You are up to something,' I whisper, but he just sticks his tongue out at me.

'No I'm not,' he says.

At three o'clock, Miss Cortez makes an announcement on the loud speaker.

'Please make your way to the roped-off area by the Square Tent for the final of the Pet Competition,' she says and everyone lines up along the ropes.

Theo checks his watch, not once, but twice.

'How much longer before we are on?' he asks Grandpa.

'About fifteen minutes,' Grandpa says and Theo checks his watch again.

'What's up with you wanting to know the time?' I whisper to him.

'None of your business,' he says, and grins. 'But it's looking good.'

Whiskey Worthington disappears inside a large tube and pops out the other end. The Pukewart and The Vomitwart lift the tube up with Whiskey still inside and the cat keeps appearing at each end waving its paws at everyone. It's quite funny and everyone claps and some people even cheer.

Then our names are called and Granddad says,

'Good luck,' as we duck under the rope and wheel the base, plank, box and trays to the middle.

When we are ready and everyone is looking at us, Natters and Theo throw their arms around like they are in the circus. Theo is grinning at everyone. He is dressed up and in his little brain he is performing on television with millions of people tuned in, just to watch him.

Goffo runs along the plank and disappears inside the yellow cardboard box.

Everyone laughs when two identical dogs are lifted out of it a few seconds later.

Theo and I carry the dogs on their trays.

We bow like sumo wrestlers, slowly lowering the trays to the ground.

Natters holds the dogs' collars while Theo and I show everyone the words on the trays.

Both dogs bark at the blue tray then head for the red one, and everyone laughs again.

Theo puts the yellow cardboard box underneath the raised see-saw plank.

Natters and I stand at the other end with one foot each on the plank to make sure it doesn't swing down when Ivan walks up it and drops into the yellow cardboard box.

Then it is Goffo's turn to walk the plank. And just as he is at the top Theo mutters,

'Goffo ... stay.'

And I frown because telling Goffo to stay at the top of the plank is not on Nana's list of instructions. But Theo is grinning to himself and Goffo is frozen and looking at Theo.

And I don't know why.

FACT NUMBER SEVENTY-NINE

I love ... my brother!

Nana would be proud because Goffo does exactly what Theo tells him and stands absolutely still, **poised like a pirate** about to drop off the plank and be eaten by sharks swimming round inside the yellow box.

'What is he doing?' Natters whispers.

'No idea,' I say.

But actually, I suddenly do.

And I want to giggle like I have caught some hormones from Natters and Janine.

At that moment I love Theo more than anything else in the world.

I know why he is wearing his watch.

I know why Goffo was down the garden when
Nana wanted to brush him.

'Stay,' Theo mutters again. And everyone is
watching, waiting, listening for the final part of
our trick.

'You can do it,' Theo says. 'Think ... pig's ears. It
is six hours three minutes since you had one. I
know it's a bit early but go on ... do it.'

'Yes, do it,' I whisper. 'Think ffffourteen. Do it in
front of Miss Cortez and Nana and everyone else.
Please, Goffo. Just for us.'

And it is like Goffo understands what we are
whispering and he looks at Theo and then turns
his head and looks at me.

And I nod and I smile at him.

And standing there at the top of the plank in
the middle of the school playing field, Goffo
sends out one of the most amazing, squelchy,
squishy, loud, smelly, revolting **farts** he has ever
done.

It is long.

It is low.

It rumbles.

It reverberates.

It stinks.

It pongs.

It wafts.

It is totally.

Utterly.

Brilliantly.

Epic.

And then he tries to catch the smell by shuffling his little body backwards down the plank.

He looks hilarious.

He has to win because everyone is laughing and clapping, even though the grown-ups think they shouldn't really find it funny.

Even Nana is laughing.

And shaking her head at the same time.

And Theo's face is one of **total amazement**.

His mouth drops open like he is surprised and embarrassed.

Then he says,

'Goffo, come back,' in a voice just like Nana's. And Goffo trots back up the plank and jumps into the yellow cardboard box. Natters and I run to stand by the box and help Theo lift it up and take a bow.

And as we do there is a tiny little wifta from the bottom of the box that only Natters, Theo and I hear.

We look inside the box.

There is not much spare room in there.

But both dogs are waving their noses and trying to shuffle backwards to catch the smell.

'Ivan only had three minutes with the pig's ear before I had to fetch him back,' Theo whispers. Then he says,

'There once was a dog called Goffo, who did a big let offo.'

And I say,

'He stood on some wood, then as loud as he could, let rip with a ... '

And it's the last line again.

And I'm stuck.

Because nothing else rhymes with offo.

But it doesn't matter, because by now we are laughing so much it hurts.

'Oi, Georgie boy,' The Pukewart whispers as we stand
up to leave assembly. 'Your dog's a freak of
nature and that girl who helped you is older
than eleven. So you cheated. They let you win
the Pet Competition because your mum's got a
brain tumour.'

Ignore him.

Ignore him.

He is a bully.

But he is talking about Mum, like she would get
a brain tumour so we can win a competition and
have a stupid article in the newspaper about us
giving the prize money to a cancer charity. And

they only found that out because Theo opened his big mouth.

Again.

The reporter also found out about Harry Worthington being The Pukewart's brother and wrote about him waiting to go to court next month in the same article.

Mum cried last night. Dad was with her all evening, sitting by her bed.

Theo and I went up once or twice to make sure she was all right.

Then we were extra quiet downstairs.

When we kissed her goodnight she turned her head towards us.

And tried to smile.

But couldn't.

The Pukewart's words become a blur as I practise in my head how to ignore him.

But suddenly I don't want to ignore him any longer and my fingers curl into a fist and when the sneer in his voice is only ten centimetres behind my left ear I open my mouth and scream. At the same time my right hand travels upwards like a rocket as I spin round.

And lands right in the middle of Carl Worthington's face.

The Pukewart *has red blood.*

Blood pours out of his nose as he **reels backwards**.

He lifts his hands up to his face.

Blood **spurts** through his fingers.

It runs like raindrops down the backs of his hands.

Inside my brain I feel totally calm.

My knuckles hurt like they just hit a hard rock.

I should not have done it.

I definitely should not have done it when we are in the hall getting ready to leave assembly and the whole school, including Miss Cortez, is watching.

Thumping someone is never ever the right thing to do.

I know I am going to be in big trouble for what I have just done.

But at this moment I do not care.

Because I am in control of something.

I decided what was going to happen.

And I am still in control because The Pukewart is now lying at my feet.

He is **whimpering like a little dog.**

And if Goffo were here, he would lift his leg and wee on him.

So would Ivan.

And Nana would say, 'Good dog,' to both of them.

The walls in Miss Cortez's office are pale grey. She is wearing silver sandals. She pulls a tissue out of the box on the small table in front of the comfy armchairs, wipes her eyes then blows her nose. Her cat is having an operation on its jaw today. She told us in assembly. It must be upsetting her.

Then she walks over to her desk and lifts the telephone receiver. A few seconds later she asks Dad to collect me from school.

I hope Theo comes home with us as well.

Dermo waves and walks over to the gate when he sees me and Theo and Dad walking through it.

'You'll be all right?' Dad says.

I nod.

I will be.

'It won't happen again, will it?' he says.

He doesn't have to keep asking me that.

It won't, if no one is nasty about Mum.

Miss Cortez and Mrs Logan know what The Pukewart said. I wrote it down on the form that goes with a red card when I was in Miss Cortez's office. When

Miss Cortez read it she asked if I had made it up. I shook my head and she said,

'Oh.'

Mrs Logan smiles when Dermo and I walk in the classroom.

So do Skye and Alice.

The Pukewart is still at home.

Recovering.

AJ **scowls**.

But he would.

I have to stay in at playtime. It is part of my punishment for **socking** The Pukewart in the nose.

So I'm making a card for Mum.

'Can I stay in and help him?' Dermo says.

'Staying in is meant to be a punishment,' Mrs Logan says.

'I want to make a card for my dad,' Dermo says. 'It's his birthday next week.'

So Mrs Logan lets us stay in together, tucked behind the cupboard with the special art club pens where no one can see us. I draw a sunflower on the front of my card and inside I write,

Dear Mum, I love you.

From, George x

I want to write 'Get Well Soon'.

But I know she never will.

FACT NUMBER EIGHTY-THREE

Mum dies at 2.45 in the morning.

The newspaper announcement reads:

Victoria Grace Warren (nee Cooper) died peacefully at St Francis Hospice on 16th August, aged 40. Much loved wife of Jack, devoted mother of George and Theo and precious daughter of Arthur and Joyce. Beloved sister of Christine and favourite aunt of Natalie Jane. Sorely missed by Albert and Elise. Goffo and Ivan loved her too. Funeral on 24th August, 2 p.m. at St Saviour's Church. No flowers. Donations to St Francis Hospice.

We stand in a line.

I am wearing my school shoes.

I am holding Dad's right hand.

Theo is holding his left.

Twelve sunflowers lie on the oak veneer coffin. Mine is the biggest so it is in the middle. The sunflowers stare at the sky and we stare at the box where Mum's body is. Inside it, she is wearing the dress with cherry blossoms that Dad bought her when they went to Japan.

Elise stands next to Grandpa. Her mummy died when she was ten as well.

Nana stands next to Granddad. He has his arm round her shoulders because she is crying. Granddad is crying too because Mum was their daughter and they loved her.

Natters is very close to Chrissie and is holding a tissue in her hand. Her black bag is over her shoulder.

Mrs Shardini is standing next to Fran who is wearing dangly earrings.

Sharon and Dermo are next to her. Like me, Dermo is wearing his school trousers.

There are lots of other people as well. I know some of them, like the lady from The Flower Shop, Matthew Draylong's mum and the man who lives the other side of Mrs Shardini. They are here to let us know they are sad too. Lots of them sent cards that are on the window sill and the mantelpiece.

I do not have a mummy any more.

She died.

Six days ago.

And today she can't give me a hug even though I miss her so much my heart feels like it is being cut in two.

Dad is here.

Theo is here.

All the other people are here.

But they are not Mum.

Next to my bed are three photographs. Dad printed them off for me.

There's one of us at Topplehurst Model Village. Mum is wearing her favourite green jumper and she is laughing and eating a cheese and pickle sandwich.

There's one of the barbecue and we are pulling silly faces at the wasp and laughing. Mum is smiling at the camera.

The last one is at Thendon Wildlife Park. Dad asked a lady with a little boy to take it when Granddad bought us ice creams. Ivan and Goffo are sitting like statues on either side of Mum's wheelchair.

It is our family.

With Mum in the middle.

The photographs are next to my Triceratops and the Goffo pencil sharpener and the emperor penguin. The mummy penguin is looking down at her baby and the baby is looking up at his mummy.

He always will.

Ethel the Great African Snail is propped up against my Arsenal lamp. Whenever I look at it I think of sitting outside the Insect and Invertebrate House the last time we played the Visiting Game.

And I know I will never play that game again.

The last line is always the hardest.

When the programme about Thendon Wildlife
Park is on the telly, we sit and watch it like when
we used to watch things Dad missed because he
was at work.

Only now it is Mum who is missing.

And there is Dad, pushing Mum's wheelchair
down the path towards the langur's cage. Theo is
next, with Nana. I am chatting to Granddad and
I know we are talking about him buying everyone
a strawberry ice cream.

Then Theo and Natters and I say how great
Thendon Wildlife Park is. And as we do, a

langur swings on to the cage just above Theo's head and starts scratching its tummy and then its bottom.

'Love that langur,' Dad says.

Then the langur **twiddles** its toes round the cage netting, hangs upside down and sticks its tongue out at the camera.

'Brilliant!' Dad says. 'My boys are on the telly and all anyone will remember about them is the langur.'

And when we have finished watching the programme and run the recording back and watched it again, we cry, together, because we miss Mum so much and wish she was still with us. Goffo gets off the sofa and walks round the room like he is looking for her. Then he sits down in front of the television waiting for her to come back on again.

So Dad fetches him a pig's ear and makes a bowl of popcorn in the microwave for us and says,

'Shall we watch sports day again as well?'

And because we want to see Mum, we do, and Theo's wellie still lands on his head.

Then we watch the Pet Competition at the Summer Showdown and Goffo still shuffles down the see-saw plank. We tell Dad about Theo giving Ivan a pig's ear and he bursts out laughing.

'Mum loved you two so much,' he says.

We loved her as well.

We still do.

And we sit in silence for a few seconds before Theo says in a really quiet voice,

'But our mum is no longer here.'

And I whisper, because the words pop into my mind,

'And we'll cry for at least a year.'

And Dad says,

'I'm hurting inside, even though I have cried.'

And he hugs us really tight. And we're all trying to think of the last line. And there are loads of words that rhyme with here and year, but none of them seem right.

None of them are about Mum.

None of them are good enough.

And then Theo says,

'There once was a lovely mum.'

And Dad says,

'That doesn't rhyme with hear and year.'

And Theo says,

'I know. It's a new one. There once was a lovely mum.'

And I say, straight away,

'Two boys came out of her tum.'

And Theo says,

'She had a dog too, who did a big poo.'

'Theo, that is so boring,' Dad says. 'Come up with something better.'

Dad and I can almost hear Theo's brain ticking over.

Then he says,

'Is Thendon Wildlife Park a zoo?'

And Dad says,

'Would you like it to be?'

And Theo says,

'Yes.'

'In that case, it is.'

And Theo says,

'She had a dog too, who went to the zoo.'

And now we're all trying to think of a last line
that rhymes with mum.

We sit there and no one says anything.

Until dad says,

'The only last line I can think of is

And we'll never forget your lovely mum.'

Which is sort of cheating because Mum is the last
word of the first line.

But that doesn't matter

Because what Dad said is right.

We never ever will forget her.

Because she'll always be.

Our lovely mum.

Acknowledgements

A host of people journeyed with me as *Us Minus Mum* unfolded.

The first paragraphs were written in Amsterdam after a morning mooching round art galleries. Thank you, Derek, for your love over many years and for going to Amsterdam, so I could travel with you and start writing this book.

Tom, Sarah, Toby and Hannah heard the first draft of the opening chapters. Thank you for listening, chuckling and encouraging. Maybe George and Theo's activities mirrored some of the things you got up to when you were children.

Liz Hale and Professor Karol Sikora helped with medical details and Dr Ann Rowland from Child Bereavement UK helped with the portrayal of the grieving process. I really appreciate the time you gave and comments you made. Thank you very much.

Thank you too to Gillian Jones, Lisa Collins and Brad for telling me about your dogs. Goffo and Ivan see Evie, Pippin and Lizzie as their role models.

Bev Reader listened patiently as the story developed and the children at Manor Farm Community Junior School constantly provided a wealth of ideas. Thank you.

Penny Holroyde at Caroline Sheldon Literary Agency believed in the manuscript sufficiently to take on a newcomer. Thank you for your support and guidance throughout the publishing process.

Thanks too to Kate Agar, commissioning editor at Little, Brown. It's been great working with you and the team – Matt Ralphs, Stephanie Melrose and Kate Webster.

My final thank you is to my sisters. We became Us Minus Mum as I wrote the book. Our mum gave us a love for words and encouraged us to be creative. Thank you, Lib, and thank you, Ro, for your love and support over the years and for being part of my journey.

If you have been affected by any of the issues in this story, the charity Child Bereavement UK has a support line on
0800 02 888 40.

Or you can go to www.childbereavement.org.uk for information.

About the Author

Heather Butler grew up in a vicarage, which meant her life was filled with a tapestry of random and interesting characters. But what influenced her most was her mum, who could create stories from thin air.

Heather is a primary school teacher. When her sons were little they often brought toys and other objects to her to be included in bedtime stories. Her sons grew older, but Heather carried on creating stories as well as leading writing workshops across the UK.

For more details about Heather and her writing, visit: www.heatherbutler.info

Reader Pack

We've asked Heather lots of interesting questions about *Us Minus Mum* and the characters she has created. One of her answers is below, but you can see more in our reader pack which also contains games and activities: www.lbkids.co.uk/heatherbutler

Q: How did you create George?

A: I was sitting on my own in a café in Amsterdam and my foot started itching. And suddenly, there was George, scratching his foot underneath the safety of his quilt while he thought about what was going on in his life. So I started writing down what he was thinking – I never go anywhere without a pen and a notebook – and what I wrote down that day became two of the facts in *Us Minus Mum.*

Later that day I wrote the part when Chrissie takes Theo and George shopping. As soon as I had created George, I knew he was going to be the narrator and that he and Theo would face Mum's illness together. George was also going to be the sensible brother, with Theo being the opposite.

RU
3/16